A HOUSE OF POWDER AND PLOT

A TALE OF LEVANTHRIA

A.P BESWICK

ISBN - 978-1-916671-14-0

Editor - Quin Nichols - Quill & Bone Editing

Cover Design - Rafido Designs.

Acknowledgments

To The Plotters

James Gordon
E.G.Collins
Connor J Harrington
Bradley Bolt
Bradley Henson
Peter Ressler
Cole Woody
Emma Atkinson
Debbie Harris
Michael Simkin
Practical Deduction
Lauren Sarah Grant Tildsley
Brenden Lowe
Nathan Coelho
Kyle Meidinger
Ben Woolven

A HOUSE OF POWDER AND PLOT

KING'S KEEP

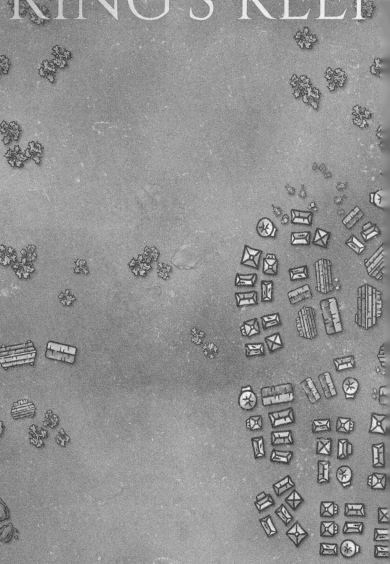

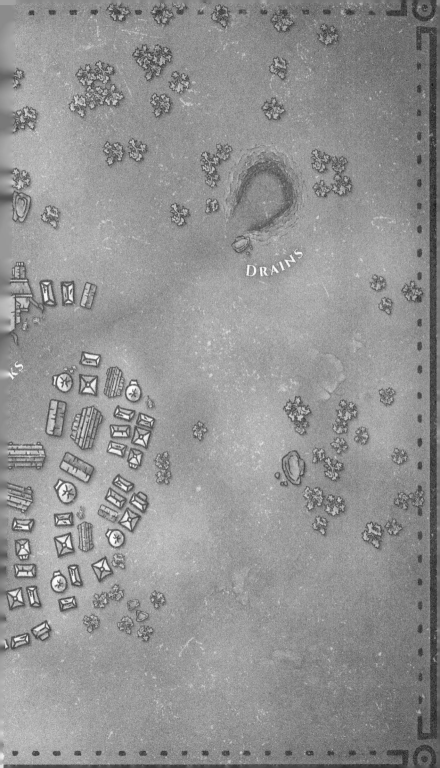

DRAINS

KS

PROLOGUE

Morvin finished grinding the thick powder. What skin lay exposed under his thick, brown beard was coated in dirt and grime. His beard, which was matted and knotted, dropped down to his lower gut, and his clothes were filthy and torn. He was a far cry from the proud Dwarf he once was. Now Morvin was a ghost of his former self, without a care for his appearance, his sole focus being that of making this blasted powder work.

When he finished grinding the powder, Morvin gave it a sniff; charcoal, twooly leaves, and narmaric made for an interesting combination, one that his notes suggested could work. The smell was like soot crossed with oats, which strangely brought about a pang of hunger in the pits of his stomach. He tipped the mortar on its side, emptying the contents of the powder onto his stained and cracked desk. Small circles of burnt wood decorated the desk's surface, a consequence of his experiments. None of which had borne the results he so desired.

Morvin reached for the contraption he had made, which

had a metallic mechanism that forced pieces of flint together to form a spark when activated.

"Here we go." Morvin pressed the mechanism to the surface of the powder and clicked it. It sparked, and Morvin's heart drummed with anticipation. Was this it, was this the one?

It was short lived, however; the flame hissed into a dry fizz before vanishing, leaving behind a rancid smell that reminded Morvin of rotten eggs.

"Blasts!" he cursed before reaching for his notebook that lay open beside him, the outer edges of which were frayed and charred. He took his quill and scribbled the combination he had used for this powder, then added a cross next to it. Above this entry were rows upon rows of scribbled combinations, concoctions, and recipes that Morvin had already tried, all of which had failed. He was determined to find the answer, however, and he would keep on trying until he created a powder that would work for his invention.

He glanced over at the invention he had been working on for so long, which sat on a plinth protruding from the stone walls of his basement. The device had a thick, elongated cylinder with a metal frame pressed around its outer edge to stabilise it. One end bore a handle carved from an aged grogoa tree, the densest wood he could find. It had been a nightmare to carve, the wood itself as hard as granite, but it was the only material Morvin had deduced would work with his contraption. Fitted above the handle of his device was a mechanism that was similar to the one he had just used to ignite a spark. The device was crafted well, but it was rough in appearance and lacked finesse. This was something he could dedicate his time to once he had got the blasted thing to work.

Letting out a groan of frustration, Morvin tossed his quill aside and brought down a clenched fist firmly onto the table. Bottles of ingredients rattled and clinked from the force before one of the bottles shattered, spilling its contents over the pile of powder that had fizzled out. As the compounds connected, a strange, deep-blue light emitted from them, as if the powder itself was glowing. Seizing the opportunity, Morvin reached for his pestle and ground the raw ingredient into the powder. He recognised it as ironite fragments straight away: the black stone was distinct thanks to the orange veins inside.

He continued to grind the powder until the entire pile was glowing. Whatever had happened, it seemed to be working. Morvin was certain that his theory was right, and he excitedly took out his mechanical flint and placed it against the surface of the powder. It ignited into a bright-white light that Morvin was only able to stare into due to the thick goggles he was wearing. His chest pounded and he held his breath in anticipation. A brighter flash of light was greeted by a pop and a crack as the powder ignited before him, sending a billow of soot into Morvin's already mucky face. He raised his goggles, revealing his clean, wide eyes, and for the first time in as long as he could remember, he smiled. He couldn't help himself as he let out an uncontrolled, deep giggle, rubbing his finger over the small hole that had formed on the table.

"That's it! It worked!" He clapped his hands together, then grabbed the mortar and pestle along with another handful of ironite ore. This time there was far more in quantity of each ingredient as he set about grinding them all together. When the glowing powder was sufficiently mixed once more, he tipped out the full mortar and started again and again until he had a large pile of glowing powder sitting on the desk in front of him.

When he was done, Morvin stepped onto his rickety old chair, which groaned under his weight as he reached over his desk to retrieve the weapon he had forged. Hopping down from the chair, Morvin raised the weighty device, one hand holding the handle and the other hand braced underneath the metal shaft.

The metal was rough against his fingers, the wooden hilt as cold as stone. Morvin examined his craftsmanship for a moment, pondering on what parts of the device he could tinker with to make it even better. His hands trembled with excitement as the deep-blue glow from the powder lit up his face. He propped the shaft of the weapon upright before using his shovel-like hands to scoop the powder inside. When he was done, he took hold of a small metal ball that he had forged previously and dropped it inside. Then he heaved the loaded weapon into his hand. But, struggling with the overall weight of it, Morvin lost his balance and staggered backwards, then forwards as he fought to regain composure.

"Here goes." Holding his breath, Morvin pulled the trigger on the flint mechanism. It sparked, triggering the brightest flash of light Morvin had ever witnessed. It was as if a star had landed in front of him. What followed was an almighty boom that echoed throughout Morvin's basement as the powder reacted to the spark. Before he had time to think, Morvin was hurled across the room from the force of the explosion. His hands seared with pain as the pressure and heat forced him to let go of the weapon. With a thud, Morvin crashed through his table, bottles of ingredient smashing onto the ground on him and around him. Dust and soot filled every space within the room, causing Morvin to cough and shake as he gasped for breath. Each breath he took caused him to cough and splutter even more as he inhaled soot. His body ached as though he had been dragged up a mountain by a wild frost troll, and his chest stung every time he took a breath. He knew straight away he had broken a rib or two but despite the pain, despite the discomfort, he could not help but let out a crazed laugh.

A draft sucked the dust from the room and Morvin was met by a cool breeze that danced over his sweat- and soot-filled face, bringing with it a freshness. As the soot gradually thinned, Morvin was able to take in the state of his basement.

It lay in ruins. His desk was destroyed, his ingredients scattered and mixed all over the floor. As he kicked broken splinters of wood and boards around the floor until he found his weapon, Morvin realised he was lucky that everything mixing on the ground had not triggered another reaction.

A throbbing sensation in his left hand caused Morvin to inspect his injury. The skin of his palm and fingers were severely burnt and charred. His flesh was singed from where he had held the metal shaft of his weapon. As the cloud of soot continued to settle, he noticed his weapon on the floor, his skin printed onto the side of it. The end of the shaft had split apart and fragmented, and the flint mechanism was gone, the wooden handle nearly detached.

The weapon had been destroyed. The time it had taken him to craft it, gone in a moment. It was not fixable by any means, but still, Morvin simply laughed, undeterred even as moonlight forced its way through the ginormous hole in the wall of his house.

Outside, shouts and cries of the other townsfolk had erupted in response to the explosion. The hole was big enough to step through, so Morvin forced his way outside, still coughing and heaving but very much happy. Once outside, he patted himself down, soot billowing and forming dust clouds around him as if he were a god in the skies. Albeit a blackened, darkened god.

One whose darkened heart would change the landscape of these lands.

I

With a thunderous knock, an iron-like fist hammered against the door, threatening to splinter the wood into pieces. Dust fell from the crumbling ceiling, landing onto Morvin's lap like heavy snow. He let out an almighty sigh, resigned to his fate. He had been waiting for this moment ever since he had blasted the hole in his basement the night before. When the second knock came, his front door barely remained on its hinges.

"Morvin Torhold!" the voice boomed from the other side. "This is Captain Malachi of the Royal King's Guard. Open the door, otherwise we will be forced to enter, by royal decree."

"Bollocks," Morvin muttered under his breath. How could there already be a royal decree given when the king was not even in these lands? Especially when it was only last night that he'd had his accident.

By the third knock, Morvin could feel his aggravation rising, and he hopped from his chair, brushing the fallen dust from his dirt-covered pants. "Blasts, I am coming!"

The brisk knocking stopped as Morvin paced to the

door and yanked it open. His gaze buried deep into Captain Malachi's as he eyed him up.

The captain wore the colours of the Royal King's Guard: a black tunic with the king's crest embroidered on the chest in gold. He looked relatively young for his rank with Morvin putting him in his mid-twenties. He stood far taller than Morvin and had bright-blue eyes that contrasted with his complexion. The rest of his head remained hidden under the hood of his cloak. He may have been taller and strongly built but this did not intimidate Morvin in the slightest.

Morvin puffed out his chest. "What do you want?"

Captain Malachi simply rolled his eyes in disdain. "Are we really going to do this?"

Morvin stood defiantly in front of the captain. "What do you want?" he repeated, his words slow and concise as if he were speaking to an imbecile.

With a laboured sigh, Captain Malachi pushed Morvin to the side and marched into the house. "Search every-where," he said, addressing the guards that followed him into Morvin's living room.

"You can't just walk in here!" Morvin protested, a flash of heat erupting in his face. He puffed up his cheeks even more and channelled all his ancestral Dwarven rage as he stepped towards the rude captain, intending to show him exactly how he felt about this intrusion.

Two guards sprang into action and took hold of his arms, gripping him tightly. Morvin was not a fighter; he was an inventor, a tinkerer. These guards, however, did not know that, and he struggled against them as he tried to intimidate them as best he could.

"I can do what I like," Captain Malachi scoffed, lowering his hood to reveal his short, blond hair. He reached inside of his cloak and revealed a scroll which he unfurled and started reading out loud. "Morvin Torhold, you are accused of the following: creating disorder and fear amongst the people of Noren, causing damage to the king's land . . ."

Morvin snorted in disgust at the sheer mention of the king, let alone the absurd notion that the tree he had decimated belonged to him.

Captain Malachi gave a dry cough before continuing, "You are also accused of being a mage and as such, have triggered Section Five, Paragraph Three of the Mage Enlistment Order as decreed by King Athos Almerion."

"I am no mage!" Morvin baulked. "Where exactly do you get your information from?"

Captain Malachi lowered the scroll and looked down his pompous nose at Morvin before walking over to the window at the far side of the room. "If that is the case, how do you explain the destruction which eviscerated the land behind your house? If not magic, what was it?"

Morvin did not reply, he just stared at the captain.

Captain Malachi turned to face Morvin once again and placed his hands behind his back, walking slowly towards the Dwarven inventor. "If not a mage," he said, leaning in close enough that Morvin could feel the heat of his breath, "what, exactly, are you?"

Morvin struggled against the tight grip on his arms, incensed by the captain's treatment of him. "Unhand me!" he demanded, pulling against the guards.

"My guards will let you go when you agree to the terms of the king's decree," he sneered. "This can end in two ways. You agree, in which case you will be free to gather your effects and say your goodbyes to any friends or family. We will return at first light, and you will be escorted by the Royal Guards to be trained for war. The second option is to be dragged from this house in disgrace and executed in front of the townsfolk of Noren for your crimes."

"Alleged," Morven said dryly.

The guards returned from downstairs and gave their captain a shake of their heads as if they could not find whatever they were looking for. Morvin had seen to that.

"Very well," Morvin lied. He knew that he would never fight in the name of the king, in this life or the next. But if he was to see his oath fulfilled, then he needed to stay alive. So with little option, he agreed to the demands being placed on him.

"It doesn't look like I have much choice," Morvin growled, his displeasure clear in his tone.

"It is if you want to hold onto your life," Captain Malachi said with a sigh. "As I said, we will be back at dawn to collect you and escort you to Askela where you will learn to harness your magic."

Morvin laughed inwardly; if only they knew that it was not magic that had caused the blast. True, magical properties had been used to cause the explosion, but Morvin held no dormant power within him that needed awakening.

"Two guards will be stationed outside in case you get any ideas about running. Know this: if you try to leave this house before we return, then you will be executed. Do I make myself clear?"

"Crystal," Morvin growled.

With a nod of the head from Captain Malachi, the two guards let go of his arms and Morvin shrugged his shoulder from their grips. His heart was pounding, and he was already evaluating the room for possible ways to escape.

"Until dawn," Captain Malachi said coldly before turning to leave with his men.

Peering out of the window, Morvin could see that one

guard had stationed himself at his front door and the other by the hole in the wall coming out of his basement. Morvin was anything but a skilled fighter, and he could not see how he could possibly escape this. However, he did have some excess powder that he could put to use.

The guard at the front door turned to see Morvin gawping at him. He looked younger than the other soldiers, but there was an anger in his eyes that was not just towards the Dwarf. Morvin feigned a nod, then grabbed hold of a bag and descended into the basement where he started rummaging around, making it look as though he was packing.

He packed his bag quickly, not with clothes or food but with his scribbled notes and as many vials of ingredients as he could. He took a chunk of dense ironite ore and placed it into his bag. It was heavy but with Morvin's Dwarven constitution, he could carry this with relative ease. The guard was keeping a steady eye on him from beyond the gaping hole that had removed half of his basement wall.

"Can I help you?" Morvin said. "Can a Dwarf not be afforded some privacy in his final moments of freedom?"

The guard was unmoved by Morvin's words and continued to watch him with an untrusting eye. Morvin had his bag packed. All he needed now was his boom pistol. He made his way back upstairs and placed his bag beside his worn armchair. The chair's colour had faded from a vibrant green to more moss-like, and perhaps that was because of the mould that had taken hold of it.

As for a plan, Morvin's boom pistol was broken beyond repair, but the guards did not know that. He knew what he was going to do: he would create a distraction using the small amount of powder that he had in his pocket and make a run for it whilst the guards were busy. It wasn't much of a plan. In fact, it was a terrible plan. But for now, it was all that Morvin had.

He moved to the kitchen area and lifted one of the floor-boards to reveal his boom pistol wrapped in a dirty cloth. He picked it up with a smile. This would go with him. After all, he could not make another without the initial proto-type. He had already been thinking of ways to improve the design.

Judging by the faintest trace of light in the sky, Morvin figured he had an hour at best before Captain Malachi returned. If he was going to do this, he would need to do it now and get a good run on the guards.

He moved to the front door and reached into his pocket, retrieving the vial with a small amount of glowing powder which he proceeded to pour behind the door. His plan was to ignite it and draw the other guard, leaving the broken wall in the basement unguarded. Then he would make his run for freedom. He didn't have speed on his side by any stretch, but what he did have was stamina. He would run across the field towards the river and travel as far north of Levanthria as his legs would carry him. After that, he had no clue what he would do, but at least he would be free from the guards, free from being a slave to the king's forces.

After emptying the vial, Morvin trailed off some twine next to his chair to act as a fuse. He hoped this would give him enough time to get downstairs before the powder ignited. Once he was in position, he leant to the side to peer out of the window and check the position of the guard.

To his surprise, no one was there.

Curious, Morvin stepped forwards to take a closer look. There was no guard at the front door, either. He pulled the door back to make certain he was not mistaken, and sure enough, no one was there. It seemed that he was free to leave.

"Is this a trap?" he mumbled under his breath. It would be too easy. His initial thought was that they were goading him into trying to leave, perhaps so they could just execute him there and then. When Morvin looked at the ground, his curiosity was piqued further: the dirt was scuffed with drag marks, speckled with what clearly appeared to be blood.

"Hello?" Morvin said to no answer. He looked out at the empty road outside his house with an untrusting glare before stepping back inside and slamming his door shut.

He ran to the back window and peered outside. The two guards lay slumped on the ground on top of each other.

This was his chance. Morvin could not afford to waste any more time. He grabbed hold of his heavy bag and tossed it over his shoulder, then picked up his boom pistol. He made for the stairs and walked down them cautiously. After all, he had no idea who to thank for the guards being removed from their posts.

When he reached the basement, he couldn't see anyone. Morvin approached the hole in the wall and climbed over the broken stone. His ankle gave way over the crumbling debris, but aside from a quick, sharp sting in his ankle, it did not deter him. As he reached the outside, his attention was brought to the two guards who were slumped on top of one another. Morvin couldn't tell if they were breathing or not, but he did not care. As he readied himself to make a run for it, his attention was brought to a figure standing in front of the damaged tree. At least a third of its trunk had shredded away from the explosion. The figure was examining the scorched wood, tracing his fingers over the surface and sniffing it. He wore a long robe with the hood pulled over his head, keeping his features hidden.

"Can I help you?" Morvin demanded. "I don't take kindly to strangers poking around my house. Especially humans."

The man turned and gave no surprise to see a thickset Dwarf stood just a few feet away from him. Morvin raised his boom pistol towards the stranger.

"You must be Morvin," the man said with a soft, well-spoken accent.

Morvin eyed the stranger, keeping his weapon pointed at him. "Not only a human, you're a mage, too." He spat on the floor in front of him and shook the weapon towards the man. "I suppose I have you to thank for this." He nodded to the two fallen guards beside him. "Whatever you want, I am not interested."

The man raised his hand, his gaze drawn towards the peculiar contraption that was in Morvin's hands. The figure then turned to inspect the splintered tree once more, and smiled as realisation seemed to dawn on him.

"The device you hold . . . That is what did this damage to this tree. It is a grogoa tree, is it not?" he asked excitedly.

"Aye, but that doesn't answer my question!" Morvin shook his weapon threateningly once more. "Why is it you trespass on my lands?"

The man jumped around and hollered loudly, clapping his hands together.

"Fantastic, this is fantastic! I have so many questions about the device you have created. You are a genius." He stepped towards Morvin and raised his hands out as if he meant to touch it. "You are just the Dwarf we have been looking for."

"Don't come any closer," Morvin threatened, shaking the contraption again.

"Please, I mean you no harm. I merely wish to speak

with you. Besides, I have no doubt that if you wanted to, you could have used that peculiar device on me already. But would I be right in assuming that it is in fact broken?"

The man lowered his hood, revealing dark skin and short grey hair, his face wrinkled and cracked – a sign of the magic he had used over his life. "My name is Tarin," he said confidently.

"Put it down," a dry, threatening voice of a woman suddenly whispered, her words like ice in Morvin's ear. She had appeared beside him out of nowhere like a shroud of smoke, and now she held a dagger to the Dwarf's throat.

She was of a slender build and cast in a darkened blue cloak. Her hood was lowered, revealing dark brown hair resting over one side of her face. The other half of her head was shaven, and her skin was as pale as ice as if she had spent her entire life living in the shadows she had just crawled from.

"The blazes, I thought you said you meant me no harm," Morvin scolded. His face reddened with anger as his words thickened with frustration.

"Skyrar means only to protect me."

"Aye, so you say, but it is me who has a blade against my throat."

"And I have a strange weapon of untold power pointed at me."

Morvin remained quiet for a moment, thinking about his options. Finally, he lowered his device until it was pointed at the ground. His big blue eyes remained fixed on Tarin, however, in an untrusting stare.

Tarin gave Skyrar a nod and she sighed before she lowered the blade from Morvin's neck.

"That blade wouldn't be thick enough to cut through

my beard, let alone my throat." Morvin grinned. "You humans and your measly weapons."

"Maybe I will test that theory next time you sleep, Dwarf," Skyrar fired back, her jaw clenched. Morvin had already managed to gnaw under her skin.

"Oh, I like her," Morvin chortled. "She has a spunk about her."

"May I ask if we could move indoors to carry on our conversation? I have a proposal for you which I would like to discuss in private. We do not have long. Hear me out and we will be on our way," Tarin said.

Morvin sighed. "Is that the only way I am going to get you two to fuck off?"

Tarin smiled, nodding. "I am afraid it is."

2

"What was that magic you used to sneak up on me?" Morvin asked whilst he poured the strong-smelling tea that had been boiling on the stove. He tipped the pot over three tankards before passing one to Skyrar and one to Tarin. Skyrar accepted the tankard but after inspecting the soot-covered rim, she didn't so much as smile before placing the drink unapologetically on a small table to her side.

"You know you can both sit down?" Morvin said.

Skyrar gave a look of disgust as she eyed his furniture. Her inability to mask her displeasure was as poor as her skill at remaining hidden was great.

Tarin inspected the tankard and politely nodded in appreciation. He hesitated for the briefest of moments before he reluctantly raised it to his lips and sipped away at the piping-hot liquid. He looked surprised to find that the thick tea actually tasted quite nice. Morvin rather liked it himself; one just needed to get over the granular texture that the soot provided.

Tarin glanced at the chairs around the room, which

were all covered in dust and soot. "If it is okay, we will stand. We have been sat riding for many a week. Forgive us for the need to stretch our legs."

Skyrar rolled her eyes and moved to one of the broken windows, pulling back the moth-eaten curtain to survey outside. Morvin knew the guards would soon return for him, but it could not hurt to have one more cup of tea before he left.

"Suit yourselves." Morvin sat down on the only padded chair in the room. A plume of dust puffed outwards as the chair groaned under his weight. "She always like this?"

"I am afraid so," Tarin said before taking another sip of tea. "Skyrar is a shadow walker, in answer to your question."

"A shadow walker? What kind of magic is that?"

"It is an Elven trait, passed down through her bloodline. Not so much magic, more so ability. When in shadows she can remain hidden, to most eyes anyway. There are still some who are able to see through the cloak. It is why when our paths crossed, I knew that she would be perfect for my quest. That is what brings me here, Morvin." Tarin examined the ramshackle room and shook his head. "To your home."

"A quest? I am no mercenary, mage." Morvin took a large glut of tea from his tankard, some of which poured down his beard and onto the floor, mixing in a strange pool with the soot.

"I had word sent to me about an explosion, so we came here to find out for ourselves. You see, I have eyes everywhere, and as an inventor, you have been of special interest to me for some time. And, lo and behold, we were greeted by yourself and that curious device you have made." Tarin's eyes fixed on the broken device which stood propped against Morvin's chair.

"My boom pistol is not for sale. Besides, you know for yourself that it is broken."

"But I presume you are building another."

"Aye, still some way to go. I need to make a few adjustments of the shaft to ensure it doesn't obliterate when it fires. Nearly lost my shoulder to the recoil, too." Morvin rotated his shoulder and grimaced from the pain. It still bore the stiffness from firing the weapon.

"Boom pistol, that is a curious name. Still, it is not the pistol that brings us here. I am more interested in the magic you have used to power it."

"It is not powered by magic, mage. I am a Dwarf. I can fight my battles with weapons forged by the strength of my own hands. I do not need magic." Morvin raised his hands in front of him and gestured with them before clenching them into tight fists. "It was not magic that caused the explosion. It was a powder."

Tarin's eyes widened as Morvin spoke. "Then it is this powder of which I wish to speak. It is exactly what we have been searching for."

"No amount of coin you offer will be enough. You can pass my message on to the captain. I am not a loyal dog, and I refuse to do the king's bidding. I have no interest in handing over my inventions," Morvin snapped. He had his own reasons for creating his weapon. Reasons which he was not ready to share with these two strangers.

"The captain?" Tarin said, his face etched with confusion. "I think you have us mistaken. I have no affiliation with King Athos. In fact, quite the opposite." Tarin gave a quaint nod to Skyrar, who hitched back the dirty veil that hung down from the nearby window once more.

"All clear here," she said with an impatient tone. "We will not have long left, Tarin. I don't know why we couldn't have this conversation in the carriage on the way out of town."

"Because Morvin needs to make his decision first," Tarin said calmly. "She is right, Morvin. we don't have long. Judging by the guards outside, I assume you agreed to enlist to their forces? I am all too familiar with their ways," Tarin said, a sudden intensity about him.

"Well, er, yes," Morvin replied, bringing a hand to the back of his head and rubbing it with a forced smile. "After the explosion, they had questions for me. Truth be told, I thought they were going to arrest me. But to my surprise, they asked me to enlist to the king's army. Said they would give me what I needed to finish my tinkering."

"And what did you say?"

"The same as what I am telling you – fuck off. Well, kind of. I told them I would join to buy me some time so I could pack my things and make a run for it." There was a sternness in Morvin's heart. He had no interest in giving away his weapon, even if it could only fire one shot. This was information only he knew.

Tarin let out an exasperated sigh and brought his fingers to his temple, massaging it gently. "I suppose you didn't have much time to formulate a proper plan. I am afraid we do not have much time to go through everything before they return. Probably even less if it has been reported that two of their guards are missing."

"Let me leave, then." Morvin stood defiantly and gave a gentle pat on the device he continued to cradle like a newborn.

Tarin stood as well. "Then all this will be wasted. Morvin, I am here to recruit you, but not to fight in the king's foolish wars." He paused, studying Morvin thought-fully. "What I ask of you is not for the faint of heart. I will speak with nothing but honesty. Once I have finished, if you are not interested in my proposal, then we will simply be on our way and you will not see or hear of us again. I do not have a vast amount of coin to offer you. Only to say, our quest leads us on a path of virtue. Some might call it vengeance."

Morvin sat forwards in his chair. "Go on."

"For too long has Levanthria struggled under the reign of King Athos, who only seeks to put power before his people. For too many years have these lands diminished under poverty, our people being forced to fight in a war which many no longer believe in. We have all had dealings with depravity since the king began his crusade. We plan on ending it, on bringing stability back to our once pros-perous lands so we can once again thrive. So we can once again live. For too long has our purpose been to serve the king in his fool's war. We have had enough, and we are going to bring it to an end."

"And how exactly do you intend to do that?" Morvin asked. "Last I knew, the king was off fighting in foreign lands against the Zarubians."

An air of nervousness came about Tarin as he hunched forwards to speak with Morvin, lowering his voice. "We are going to travel to Zarubia, Morvin. And once we are there, we are going to kill King Athos Almerion."

Silence greeted both of them as the gravity of Tarin's quest was laid bare. Skyrar shuffled nervously in anticipa-tion as she continued to watch by the window. Morvin knew they were almost out of time.

"You – you want to kill the king?" Morvin stammered. This was not how he saw the conversation going. If the wrong people heard him speak such words, they would be executed on the spot for treason. He found himself lost for words, suddenly wondering once again if this was some sort of trap.

"This magic you wield – sorry, this powder you have somehow created," Tarin corrected himself when Morvin scowled at him. "I believe it is key to us being able to do this. You see, everyone I have recruited so far has a certain skill set, something that on its own will not bring about success to my plan. But collectively, I believe that we will be able to fulfil this quest and bring about it a new age to Levanthria."

Morvin picked up his boom pistol and sat back in his chair as he gathered his thoughts. He held it in his arms as if it were a babe.

At that moment, the door splintered open with a bang, revealing a furious Captain Malachi in the doorway.

"What is the meaning of this treachery?" The captain's eyes darted from Morvin, to Tarin, then to Skyrar, who stood beside the door. His sword was already drawn, and he swung this at Skyrar, but she disappeared in a puff of smoke and reappeared beside Tarin.

"I thought you were keeping watch!" Tarin gave Skyrar an accusing stare.

"I can have a bit more fun this way." She smiled as guards flooded the room, roaring with anger and weapons drawn.

Skyrar shot forwards and sliced against the guards who one by one fell as the captain lunged towards her with his sword. He was faster than the others and slipped through Skyrar's attack. Tarin only just pulled Morvin out of the way of a strike that would have likely cleaved him in half.

Tarin's hands glowed as he muttered an incantation

under his breath. Morvin watched as magic pulsated from his palms, propelling the captain backwards towards the doorway. His power knocked the other guards to the floor too, but somehow Skyrar remained unaffected. She knelt down and with a flick of her dagger, cut the throat of the nearest guard.

"We best make our exit, Skyrar. This way," Tarin said. He was still calm but there was an assertiveness to his tone that Morvin had not noticed before.

"Hang on, I can buy us some more time," Morvin said. He reached down and grabbed hold of the twine, then pulled out his flint device and clicked it to ignite the wire. Smiling maniacally, he dropped it to the floor, eager to see if his experiment would succeed.

"Run!" he said as the lit twine moved towards the small pile of powder by the door. The three of them vaulted down the stairs and made their way outside through the basement.

"This way," Skyrar said, "the cart is around here."

An earth-shattering boom erupted as the front of Morvin's house exploded and started to crumble. Morvin was taken aback by how powerful the blast had been, given how little of the powder he had used. It was as if an earth-quake had struck as his house began to collapse. Morvin did not have time to lament the sentimental value the place held; they needed to escape and they needed to escape now.

Morvin followed Skyrar and Tarin to what he assumed was their horse and cart on the other side of the street. A plume of dust and debris had cast out around Morvin's home. He couldn't see the guards, but he could hear their groans of pain, and even he was surprised that anyone could have survived that blast. He hopped into the back of the cart as Tarin whipped the reins, and they began to barrel down the street. People were flocking from their houses to see what all the commotion was as they made their escape from Noren.

Morvin took one last look at the Kragoan Mountains that towered behind the only home he had never known.

Then he turned his sights forward.

3

Weeks passed, but Morvin spoke very little to his new companions. The rough ground of the Biterian Plains and Gondoron Pass proved particularly difficult to navigate, but they made it to the mountains to the north of Loch Bragoa, south of the kingdom of Askela, without too many hiccups. That was good; Morvin was not sure he could handle any more obstacles thrown his way after losing his home, along with any memories it had stored for him.

Tarin usually sat up front with Skyrar, the two of them alternating control of the carriage they rode in. Morvin spent his days nestled in the back of the cart, which they had filled with bottles of ingredients for him to make his powder. On his lap sat a heavy object wrapped in cloth, and inside it was his latest attempt at making a boom pistol. It was even heavier than the last one, but Morvin hoped that the thicker cylinder would prevent it from exploding at the end like the last one.

At night, they would set up camp by their carriage

whilst Skyrar kept watch, choosing to catch up on sleep whilst they travelled during the day.

"Here, have this. You must be hungry." Tarin passed Morvin a cob of bread by the open fire that they all sat around one evening. They had ridden all day, only stopping when they reached the far side of the Biterian Plains. The ground was coarse and uneven, making sitting in the back of the cart particularly uncomfortable for Morvin, whose shoulders were as tense and tight as a rock. Every bump reminded him of his broken ribs, though thankfully they had begun to heal as time passed.

Morvin's stomach let out a gurgle of anticipation as he reached across to accept the bread from a smiling Tarin.

Skyrar sat on the top of the cart, her eyes fixed onto the shrouded darkness that surrounded them, her bow sat across her lap. She had remained equally as silent as Morvin for much of the journey, and as he studied her defensive watch position, he noticed her unapproving eyes also watching him.

"Thank you," Morvin said, taking a bite from the bread. It was stale and crusted, but he didn't care. It was a feast compared to what he had been accustomed to eating of late. He ate the bread a little too quickly, needing to cough to dislodge the thick wedge that had stuck in his throat.

"Steady on, friend," Tarin chortled as he passed Morvin a flask of water, which the Dwarf hastily glugged to help clear his throat.

Skyrar simply sighed and shook her head before turning back to her watch.

Tarin was sitting on the ground against a large boulder that lay sunk into the ground, protecting him from the dirt that sprayed from the passing wind. He wore a smile of fascination as he watched Morvin eat and drink. Though his eyes were sunken and tired looking, he looked as though he still had energy within him.

"You look relaxed for someone who plots to kill the king," Morvin said with a grumble, smacking his lips together as his dry mouth was eased by the warm water.

"With your help, yes."

"Well, there is no doubt a price on my head now after what happened in Noren." Morvin had never taken a life before, but he was certain that he had now, following that blast. And even though the guards that were descending on him had been there to demand either a life of servitude or his execution, the burden of being a killer threatened to bring back up the bread he had just eaten.

"True, you are a wanted man," Tarin replied. "The rest of us are unknown. You see, I have been building my plan for some time now, recruiting the right people." He paused for a moment and smiled at Skyrar, then looked back at Morvin. "With the right skill sets."

"Why is it you need me?" Morvin asked. "I mean, I know it is my powder that you need, but why me?"

"Because you are the man behind the powder. You have invented something that the world cannot begin to comprehend. If I am honest, I cannot comprehend. How much powder did you use to create the explosion at your house?"

Morvin shrugged. His shoulders felt heavy and his body ached. "I dunno, maybe a handful. It was the last of what I had."

"Yet it yielded so much destruction." The campfire crackled as the light from the flames reflected in Tarin's dark eyes.

It was the level of destruction that worried Morvin. He had been hesitant to discuss it until now, as he had spent their journey silently grappling with the chaos and death he had caused during their escape. "I created the powder by accident," he said. "I needed a property to help power my boom pistol." Morvin cast his eyes at the ground in front of him where his destroyed weapon sat, barely held together now. "I didn't intend for it to be so potent."

"It is a truly fascinating contraption." Tarin stared at the boom pistol as if he were a ravenous beast stalking its prey. "May I?"

"Go on," Morvin said hesitantly. He could tell that Tarin had been itching to lay his hands on the device since they left Noren, but had maintained his distance out of respect. "If I am honest with you, it is not much use now. The blasted thing disintegrated as soon as I used it for the first time."

Tarin leant forwards and picked up the boom pistol. "It's heavy," he said with surprise.

"Aye, what do you expect? The thing is made of metal and grogoa wood."

Tarin manoeuvred the boom pistol in his hands, examining every detail. "And this bit –" he flicked his thumb over the flint mechanism. "This flint is what is needed to ignite the powder?"

Morvin nodded.

"Fascinating." Tarin handed the device back to Morvin.

"It best be worth it," Skyrar hissed. "We have risked everything to be here, to find you."

"It is a risk worth taking, Skyrar," Tarin said diplomatically.

"Is that true?" Morvin asked.

Tarin simply nodded.

"Why?"

"As I said back in your home, I have eyes and ears in a

lot of places, and I have been recruiting a team to help me in my quest to free Levanthria. Your peculiar skills and this powder you have created garnered my attention. It is a journey I am glad we took."

"Not all of us feel that way," Skyrar growled, her hostility causing Morvin to feel like he may need to rest with one eye open. He had received nothing but sulking glares from her ever since they left Noren, though he could not imagine what he had done to deserve it.

"When I told you of our intention to kill the king," Tarin began slowly, "you did not react like most would. Better still, you are now sitting in our company, a fugitive of the crown, of Morgana and the King's Guard. Many a man –"

Morvin gave Tarin a hard stare.

"Sorry, many a Dwarf would have taken their chances and enlisted in the army for self-preservation. Yet you did not. Why was that, Morvin?"

Morvin felt himself being pulled into a darkened void as he stared blankly back at Tarin, his thoughts pulling him back through his own past, to a better time. Before he had lost everything he held dear.

"That," he said, "is something I am not willing to share with you. Don't know if I ever will."

More days turned to nights as they continued to travel, Tarin remaining the more welcoming of the party. Skyrar had little words for Morvin other than criticism. If Morvin was being honest, she wasn't much nicer to Tarin, either, but he had noticed that she did do whatever she was asked by the mage, at least.

Morvin's head bobbled as they hit rocky terrain, jarring

him awake from his latest nap. He had never travelled for so long or been so far away from Noren. Drool hang from the corner of his mouth, dampening his thick beard. He wiped his sleeve across his mouth and looked above at the sun which beat down hard on them. Mountains flanked them on either side of the road, reaching high into the clouds above. Water ran down the tallest one, as if the gods themselves used the mountains to pour water into the nearby lakes. It was truly beautiful, and having been isolated in his ramshackle home for longer than Morvin cared to admit, he savoured nature's beauty. It was amazing to him what it could do when left to its own devices. It truly was a thing to behold.

He let out a yawn that would scare off even a borax bear, then stretched out his arms and rested his hands behind his head.

"We there yet?" he asked.

"By the gods, Morvin," Skyrar sighed, "if I have to hear you ask that question one more time" –

"Skyrar," Tarin interrupted, "our new friend is not as well travelled as you or I. You can forgive him for being less versed in the distance between towns and how long it takes to travel. You will be pleased to know, Morvin, that we are in fact here. If you look ahead, you will be able to see where we have made our camp."

Morvin arched his back and let out another loud yawn before heaving himself up to peer over Tarin's shoulder and down the valley. True to Tarin's word, at the foot of the mountain, a small plume of smoke could be seen rising into the air, a small formation of trees allowing them to be hidden.

"Why did you make your camp here?" he asked, taking in a big breath of air through his nose. It had been refreshing these past weeks to take in fresh air outside the soot-filled confines of his house. It was something he could get used to.

"Not many venture this far south. The lands are barren, and the waters of Loch Bragoa are tainted and corrupted with waste."

"That, and the beast of Bragoa is said to walk these lands every five years seeking revenge for her clan which was slaughtered." Skyrar beamed as if this thought delighted her. It was as animated as Morvin had seen her. "Or so people say, if you believe in that kind of thing," she added.

"Sounds like nothing more than an old wives' tale, designed to scare babes," Morvin said. "There are many a person who walk Levanthria that I would consider a monster, but I do not believe that such creatures exist other than in stories."

"Then you will have nothing to fear when we make our camp," Skyrar snapped before folding her arms and scouting ahead.

"Story or not, it has helped us keep a low profile whilst we have stockpiled our resources," Tarin said. "It has proven a good position for the pirate captain we have employed to gather what we need from foreign lands in preparation for our quest."

"A pirate captain, you say? That is interesting," Morvin said. "What name do they go by?"

"His name is Ulrik Thatch, a man with a thick black beard that would rival your own. He travels with a witch and their first mate." Tarin hesitated, as if calculating his next words. "Watch your tongue around Ulrik, though."

"Why?"

"He can be a bit . . . temperamental."."

31

"That is good to know. And where do they make port? I see no boat on the horizon."

"Further south, beyond those trees. *Esara's Revenge* is anchored in a cove there."

"Sounds like a ship fit for a ghost story, just like Skyrar's," Morvin teased.

"The beast of Bragoa is no laughing matter," Skyrar replied. "I swear I heard the siren singing once."

Before Morvin could goad her further, Tarin continued, "It is via their ship that we will travel west towards Zarubia. I will go into details of the plan once we have arrived at the camp and rested. Besides, there are the rest of the group that you need to be introduced to. A strange bunch, they are."

"I look forward to it," Morvin said, and he meant it. He had been alone for a long time. "I will also have to set about making my powder. I would be best preparing this before we travel by ship. I still do not fully know just how volatile this substance is."

The three of them continued exchanging conversation as they made their way down the valley. When they reached the outer edge of a small woodlands, the smell of freshly cooked meat brought a growl from Morvin's stomach that reminded him just how hungry he was.

"You can't be ready for food already, we have already eaten breakfast," Skyrar snapped as if she took personal offence.

"I may be short, lass, but us Dwarves have a strong constitution. We require food a plenty to stay strong and healthy."

"There was me thinking you did not give two shits about being healthy," Skyrar sniped back. "Tarin, when we get there, can you please make him bathe?"

Morvin stood and glowered at Skyrar. "Why don't we stop this cart and have a conversation about your manners?"

Skyrar simply laughed, waving away Morvin's offer.

"That's enough, you too," Tarin said, shaking his head in despair. "What we are going to be doing is no easy task, and you too are going to need to learn to work together if we are going to succeed. We are here now." Tarin guided the horses into a small opening in the trees. In an instant, the beautiful backdrop of mountains and flowing water was replaced with that of the greens and browns of the forest.

The smell of smoke grew stronger until collective words from a small group could also be heard blended with the chirping of the birds in the trees.

"Is there anything else that lives in these woods other than birds?" Morvin asked, shrinking into his usual proud, strong frame.

"What's the matter, you scared of a little wildlife?" Skyrar grinned an antagonistic smile and Morvin puffed himself up once more.

"Still, that does not mean we are not wise enough to be aware of any wee beasties that may be out there!" Morvin said.

Morvin found himself staring into the trees. As woodlands went, this area was not thick with leaves and shrubs. Slender trees rose high to give a sheltered canopy above but from the ground, the space was open, meaning one could see anyone approaching from a distance.

He wondered if Herelda and Korvin had been able to experience such beauty in their travels. He hoped they had. The thought of Herelda gazing upon the beauty of the valley almost brought a smile to his face – but his expression quickly faltered. He should have been experiencing this together with his wife and son, not with strangers. They should have explored the world together. It was what they had wanted, before everything happened.

The carriage hit a large rock, jolting Morvin from his darkening thoughts.

He found the smell of the woodlands discomfiting and could not hide the displeasure in his face. "We are not built for the woods. This is a home for Wood Elves, not Dwarves. Give me the smell of a burning furnace and freshly mined stone any day." Morvin already missed his home, the comfort that he found within it.

"Relax, my friend," Tarin said as he slowed the cart down. "These woodlands have offered us the shelter we have needed for some time. We will not be here long, and I can see that our comrades are still in good spirits."

Morvin peered over Tarin's shoulder to see the camp ahead of them. Four people stood to greet them, their conversation stopping at their arrival.

"Took your time," a stocky, middle-aged man said. His head was wrapped in a navy-blue bandana, and an eye patch sat over his left eye, his cheek gashed with a deep, purple scar.

"I rather thought we made good time, Darmour," Tarin said. "Tell me, were you able to gather the last of the supplies we needed?"

"Aye, we were." Darmour walked to the cart and offered a hand to help Skyrar down.

"Ever the gentleman," Skyrar laughed, then hopped down of her own accord.

The man grinned. "What are we in this world without our manners?"

"I never thought I would meet a pirate, let alone one to

hold manners," Morvin said as he eyed up Darmour suspiciously. "Are you not all meant to be scoundrels?"

Darmour laughed. "And I've never seen a Dwarf settle down away from the mountains." He reached up to where Morvin was standing in the cart and offered a handshake, which Morvin accepted. Even by his standards, the firmness of Darmour's grip was impressive.

Tarin beamed. "Let me introduce you all to Morvin," he said as he stepped down wearily from his side of the cart, gesturing for Morvin to join him. Morvin hopped off and followed Tarin towards the others.

"Meet our merry band with a shared disapproval for the king. You have already been acquainted with Darmour, first mate of *Esara's Revenge*. And this is Zerina."

In front of Morvin stood a young woman with hair as dark as the night itself. She wore leather pants, a black corset, and a black jacket tinged with blue. Her ocean-blue eyes and light-skinned cheeks were wrinkled with a kind, welcoming smile.

"Welcome, Morvin, it is a pleasure to meet you." Her voice was soft as she nodded her head towards him.

"Zerina is the most powerful sorceress I have met in these lands. One that could rival even Morgana," Tarin said.

Morvin had no clue who this Morgana he spoke of was. His life had been sheltered for the last three years since the death of his wife and son.

"Tarin, you know I prefer the term 'witch'. That is more attuned to my legacy than a spellcaster." There was a flash of displeasure from Zerina, her nose flaring as she corrected Tarin. The sudden change in her demeanour contrasted sharply with the pleasant and polite lady that had greeted them.

"You have my apologies, Zerina. It was but a simple slip

of the tongue," Tarin replied, unfazed by her reaction. "Next up is Vorax, an Elven warrior whose strength is unrivalled in these parts of the world."

Morvin had to take a step back to look up at the giant that stood before him. She held a colossal, powerful frame and was adorned in silver armour seen only by those who held a rank of knight or higher. The breastplate bore emblems that Morvin was unfamiliar with, and he could not help but gawp at her, taken in by her unforgiving, ice-blue eyes. Her light-brown hair was cut short, her pointed ears the only thing that alluded to her Elven heritage.

"Beautiful." The words left Morvin's mouth before he had time to think, and he shuffled about awkwardly to correct himself. "I mean, the armour," he amended, not being entirely honest. To him, looking at such a powerful woman was like being in the company of a god. Maybe she was of mixed heritage between an Elf and a giant. She was the biggest person Morvin had ever laid eyes on. What's more, Morvin had never expected he would find an Elf beautiful. He had always heard they were a scrawny, self-righteous race, and Skyrar had done nothing but confirm that for him. Vorax, however, seemed like something else entirely. Her strength undeniably reminded him of his late wife, Herelda, although they couldn't have been more different in appearance. Guilt ate away at his core as if he had betrayed Herelda by looking at another woman this way, especially an Elven one.

Vorax laughed and lowered herself, offering her hand to Morvin which he quickly accepted. "Don't let Tarin fool you that it is only strength that I offer. I, for one, believe that our minds are our greatest weapon." She winked at him and Morvin felt a flash of red in his cheeks.

"Strength and brains," Morvin repeated. "Tarin, where did you find this one? It is a pleasure to meet you, Vorax."

She smiled. "You too, Dwarf."

"And who might you be?" Morvin asked the last figure in the party.

The man's arms were folded, an untrusting scowl buried deep within a sea of a thick, black beard. The red of a bandana sat beneath the tricorn hat that rested on his head. There was an anger in his eyes as ferocious as the storms that he had likely weathered out at sea.

The man growled, eyeing up the Dwarf in front of him. "We do not have time to be paraded like whores at a buffet line."

Morvin laughed. "Angry bastard, aren't you?"

"This is Ulrik," Tarin explained. "Captain of *Esara's Revenge* and one of the most feared pirates not just in Levanthria, but around the world. Many have come across the blackened sails of *Esara's Revenge* but only few remain to tell the tale."

"Can we quit with the small talk?" the young captain demanded. "The ship has been ready and prepared for days now. Had you been much longer, we might have set sail without you."

"And we both know that you would have failed," Skyrar said, picking the dirt from her nails as she leant against the cart.

Morvin smiled, realising that it was not only he who she sought to wind up. She seemed to like challenging anyone.

Ulrik brought his hand to the hilt of his cutlass. "How about I remove your tongue, Elf?" he growled.

"How about we all calm down?" Zerina interjected.

"Ulrik, I do not know why you rise to Skyrar's words. You should know by now what she is like."

"We all know that Ulrik would fight with his shadow if he was given the opportunity," Skyrar fired back, unintimidated by Ulrik's threats.

Morvin could not decide whether it was bravery or stupidity that she showed. Ulrik seethed at her words, the aggression emitting from him as clear as the smoke that rose from the fire behind them.

"I don't have time for this shit!" Ulrik stepped forwards, ready to draw his blade, but was stopped in his tracks by a firm hand on his shoulder.

"Let's not lose our heads," said Vorax. There was a commanding presence in her voice; she was not asking Ulrik, she was telling him.

"Let us go for a walk, clear our heads. It has been a busy few weeks preparing the ship for our voyage." Zerina took hold of Ulrik's hand and stared deep into his eyes. "Our enemy is out there, Ulrik, not in this camp."

Ulrik breathed heavily for a moment before letting go of the hilt of his blade and shrugging his shoulder from Vorax's grasp. "Hold me like that again and I will take your hand," he told her before marching away from the camp.

"Ulrik," Zerina groaned, rolling her eyes. Ulrik didn't acknowledge her as he continued to trudge away. "Ulrik!" she repeated, following him.

"He always like that?" Morvin asked Vorax who seemed to find entertainment in the confrontation. "Believe it or not, that is him actually being quite polite by his standards." She smiled. "Come, we have prepared food."

"Oh good, I'm starving." Morvin barged past everyone straight to the fire, where what looked to be a small hog cooked on a spit awaited.

Skyrar rolled her eyes. "All he does is fucking eat!"

~

It was the nicest meal Morvin had had in years. Darmour had managed to make a glaze from ingredients sourced from the woodlands, including honey from a beehive he had stumbled upon. It gave the pork a sweet taste that Morvin had never experienced before.

"I have found that the best way to a crew's heart is through good food," Darmour said with a wink. Morvin could understand why; in that moment, he would have happily done anything that Darmour asked of him, such was his contentment.

A calm silence settled over the group as they ate, and Morvin decided it was time to get some answers.

"What is the plan then?" he asked, finishing the shredded hog. "To kill the king?"

Tarin swallowed the last of his meal before wiping the fat that had matted into his beard with the sleeve of his tunic. All eyes turned to him expectantly, and he cleared his throat. "As things stand," he began, "King Athos Almerion and his forces are at the weakest they have been in a long time. They are camped deep within Zarubia where they have taken control of a bastion. They have remained there for the last six months. The king, it is said, is rarely seen. He has become paranoid, which has made him reckless."

"Reckless," Morvin muttered. "Is that what they are calling it?"

"I have a contact there. They, like us, want to see that the king's reign ends, to allow a period of recovery for the people of Levanthria, and with that, prosperity. The king's bastion has become somewhat of a stronghold. He only lets a select few people to enter in and out of the fort, with the rest of the soldiers camped on the periphery. Our task is to infiltrate the camp. My contact will help us with that part. Once inside, we will scout the keep in the centre of the bastion. Then we will find and assassinate the king." Tarin spoke with a steely conviction that Morvin had not yet witnessed.

"You make it sound so easy," Skyrar hissed.

"I agree with the lass, we need more information than this." Morvin had so many questions, he did not know where to begin. And if he was going to set foot on a ship and sail away from his homeland, he needed to know more.

Tarin smiled, leaning towards the fire. "It is not going to be easy. In fact, it will be near impossible, but between us all, I believe we have the right tools to succeed."

Tarin looked at Skyrar. "Your rare Elven bloodline grants you the ability to shadow walk, a skill that when combined with your excellent lockpicking skills, will help us gain access." His eyes shifted around the fire to Vorax. "Vorax, the strongest and most skilled warrior. Every party needs someone with her skill with an axe. She will be key to keeping the party alive."

Next his eyes fell on Darmour. "Like myself, Darmour is a master tactician and first mate to Ulrik. He knows this plan inside out, so if anything were to happen to me, he would be able to take the reins."

Sat next to Darmour was Zerina, upon whom Tarin's eyes fell next. "Zerina has unlocked the power of the sacred waters of Treventine, waters worth more than any gold or jewels this world can offer. The Fountain of Youth. In doing so, her magic is unrivalled. You are sitting in the presence of one of the most powerful witches the world has ever seen."

Zerina gave a coy smile. She didn't look like an all-powerful witch to Morvin, but then again, he had never seen a witch before. She did, however, seem too kind and considerate to be in on such an assassination attempt.

"And are you okay with all of this, with this plan?" Morvin asked, directing his question to her.

"I swore an oath to protect Ulrik," Zerina replied quietly. "It is them who are intent on this mission."

"Speaking of Ulrik, what is his role in all of this?" Morvin asked.

"Ulrik's role in all of this is one of the most important ones. You see, the feared pirate captain possesses the magic of glamour."

"Glamour magic?" Morvin said, lowering his eyebrows. He had never heard of such a term.

"Ulrik possesses the ability to change the appearance of an item so that it looks like one thing when it is in fact another. This is going to be key to our plan." Tarin gave a large smile, the shadows cast on his face giving him a sinister look as his attention moved towards Morvin.

"Which brings us to you and your powder. How else could we smuggle such a thing into a bastion? Ulrik's magic is key, as is your powder. The rest of us are here to make sure that the powder makes it inside the king's keep."

Skyrar looked at Morvin and gave a sarcastic exploding gesture with her hands, complete with a sound effect.

Morvin grinned. He could not resist a good explosion.

Especially if it involved killing the man he hated most in this world.

4

The next day, Tarin sat in deep conversation with Darmour as Morvin climbed up the back of the cart and pulled back a thick cloth. Underneath sat vials and bottles of ingredients, supplies, his broken boom pistol, as well as a handful of tools that he would need to help him craft and tinker. In the corner sat a wooden box, its outer edges lined with metal studded strips. Morvin wanted to work on the boom pistol itself, but for now he needed to set about making some of the powder that Tarin had recruited him for.

Morvin scooped up the bottles and vials of ingredients into one of his arms, then grabbed a large rock of ironite with his free hand. He searched the area around the cart until he found a rare, thick stump, most likely from a tree felled by Vorax. He decided that this would be a good spot to work.

He dropped the stone to the side and placed the bottles and vials on the thicker grass on the opposite side of the stump before returning to the cart for some of his tools. As he collected his hammer, mortar, and pestle, he peered around the cart at Darmour and Tarin who continued to converse in hushed tones. They were not close enough for Morvin hear them, however.

He then noticed Skyrar sat by a tree just behind them, watching him intently. Morvin gave her a sly wave and a sarcastic smile. He found himself greeted by Skyrar's finger which caused him to laugh to himself as he returned to the tree stump to set about making his powder. Tarin had still not told him what he intended to do with it, only that they would need plenty of supply.

First, he needed to work on the ironite ore, one of the toughest materials in its raw form. Luckily he had the strength and constitution to make this into smaller chunks, even though he himself knew this would take him hours. And so he lowered his goggles over his eyes and set about bringing his hammer down on the stone, over and over again. For three hours he worked the stone, manoeuvring it, working on the weaker edges as the rock crumbled slowly under each heavy blow. His arms ached, and his face and beard were wet with sweat as he hammered and hammered at the stone, each blow reminding him of why he was doing this, the revenge that he sought.

At home, Morvin would often go for days on end without sleeping, simply working on his boom pistol, sketching up drawings to make the next one even better. Or at the very least being able to fire more than one shot before being rendered useless. Such was Morvin's focus that he had no idea what the other members of their party were doing, even choosing to work through the growls that emitted from his stomach as his body ached for more food. He had created a good rhythm with the stone and he did not want to disrupt this. He often found the repetitive echo of his blows soothing.

This was metal against stone, however, not metal on metal, and there was no gruelling heat of a forge to contend with. The air felt somewhat cooler than he was used to working under. By the time the last section of the raw ironite had crumbled, Morvin let go of the hammer and let out a roar of pain tinged with joy from having finished the task. His hand cramped as he did so, and he stretched out his fingers, consciously fighting as his muscles contracted and tried to pull his fingers inwards. His forearm felt as though he had shoved it into the flames of a fire, such was the deep burn.

When he looked up, he was surprised to find that dusk was creeping in on him. He had barely noticed the setting sun, which was now sinking behind the canopy of trees above, bringing with it a darkness. He clenched and unclenched his fist as he allowed his tense muscles to relax, surveying his day's work. A pile of crumbled stone sat on the tree stump and lay scattered around its base.

Happy with his progress, Morvin stretched out his back and made his way over to the camp, where Darmour, Tarin, Vorax, and Skyrar sat around the open fire. A gentle glow lit up their faces as Darmour tended to a delightful-smelling stew. A large pile of cut logs sat beside Vorax, who tossed one into the fire as Morvin approached.

"How have you gotten on?" Tarin asked. "We did not wish to disturb you. I have never seen focus like that."

"I think I am going to be able to hear that blasted hammer in my dreams!" Skyrar sniped.

Morvin laughed, raising his hand to the back of his head. "Do you have any idea how tough ironite is, child?"

Skyrar shook her head. "What, do you want a trinket or something?"

"The stone is broken down. With that amount of ore, I

reckon I will be able to have a barrel of powder by the morning."

"That soon? That is impressive. Do you not need to rest?" Tarin asked, accepting a bowl of stew from Darmour.

Darmour handed Morvin a bowl of food as he took up a seat around the campfire. After breathing in the alluring fragrance, he said, "Us Dwarves are not as weak as you humans. We can go for days without sleep." He raised the wooden bowl to his nose and allowed the aroma to warm his lungs. The meaty smell of thick gravy graced him, causing his hunger to rise. He raised the bowl and sipped it as if it were a tankard of ale. It tasted even nicer than it smelled.

"You, sir, are a mage when it comes to food," Morvin said to Darmour. Smiling, he poured the bowl into his mouth and the juices of the meat and stew billowed in, trickling down his beard in the process.

"Thank you," Darmour said, passing bowls to Skyrar and Vorax. He then filled three more, keeping one for himself. "It is the leftover hog from earlier, along with some vegetables and herbs that I foraged whilst you were busy at work."

"There was leftovers?" Morvin joked before finishing his stew.

"Don't worry, there is more in the pot, help yourself. I dread to think how much food you need to keep working like you have done this afternoon. I have never witnessed a Dwarf at work before, and I daresay, I am impressed." Darmour smiled as he drank his stew, and for a few minutes, there was a comfortable silence whilst the group finished their meal.

"Right, I best fetch this back to the ship. Knowing Ulrik, he will be there with Zerina." Darmour placed his dish by the fire and picked up the other two bowls. "See you later." He nodded to the group before heading off into the darkness.

"Is it safe for him to travel alone?" Morvin asked. "It would be a dreadful waste if he was to get an end." Now that Morvin had tasted his food, he looked forward to meal-times with the group.

"Do not worry, friend, As good as Darmour is at cook-ing, he is even better with a blade." Tarin finished his stew and placed his bowl onto one of Darmour's. "As much as I appreciate his good cooking, it is his ability in battle that makes him invaluable to this group."

"I will have this powder ready by morning," Morvin said. "What is it that you intend to do with it?"

"This is something I will be more than happy to go through with you once we set sail. Besides, we will have time to pass. For now, if you may focus on creating that powder."

"Must you always speak in riddles, old man? Why can't you just share what your plan is?" Skyrar snapped. "It can't be for that fucking boom pistol, as it's clearly useless once it has been fired." She tossed her empty bowl on the ground in front of her. "You ask us to follow you, to assassinate the king, yet all we have to go off at the moment is this powder and hushed words shared between yourself and Darmour. It is as if you do not trust us."

"It is not a question of trust, Skyrar. I need to make sure the plan is sound. When I know this, I will go through it with you all, in detail. What is important is that each of you remember the detail, for there is a specific reason I have recruited each and every one of you to our cause." Tarin stood and yawned. "Now if you don't mind, I am to retire. The travelling has taken it out of me. Morvin, know that the sooner that powder of yours is ready, the sooner we will be able to travel."

"I'll get to work right away." With this, Morvin headed back to his makeshift workstation and set about mixing the ingredients together. If he worked through the night without a rest, he would hopefully have the powder finished by sunrise. And he would be another day closer to avenging his fallen family.

5

Darkness surrounded Morvin as he ground the glowing substance into a fine powder with the mortar and pestle. It had again been a number of hours since he set to work, and once again, his forearm ached from his labours. The powder glowed white, illuminating the area immediately in front of him. An old oak barrel beside Morvin also shone where he was pouring the powder into.

No fire burned behind him as he worked, and although his muscles ached and burned, the cold of the night was beginning to take hold of him. He sniffed up his running nose as he continued to grind the ingredients into a fine dust before inspecting it and pouring it into the barrel carefully. He had seen how volatile the powder was in his own home. The force that it wielded was truly incredible for such a small amount, so Morvin did not want to risk any burning embers floating by and triggering an explosion.

Once Morvin had tipped the powder into the barrel, he peered over the side to take a look. It was filled to around a quarter of the way up. Morvin sighed, knowing it was going to be a long night if he was to have everything ready for their impending departure.

Something rustled in the trees nearby, and Morvin stopped in his tracks. He stared into the darkness as an eery silence fell over the camp.

There was another rustle of grass, and Morvin jumped back before a white and grey hare hopped into the circular glow around him that the powder had created. Then a strange noise flowed through the trees. It was a hymn-like song, as if the gods sang playfully above them. The alluring sound pulled at the pit of his stomach, and suddenly he felt a strong temptation to leave the camp and follow it. He found himself falling into a trance-like state where he even started humming the tune back.

"Are you okay?" Vorax asked from behind, snapping Morvin from his reverie.

"Did you hear that?" he asked, but the strange noise stopped as fast as it had started.

"No, but I know it will be that of the siren that lives in the cursed waters of the lake. Story says that the she lures people to her darkened waters with her siren's song."

Morvin shuddered. Had Vorax not interrupted his thoughts, he would have happily followed the song to its source and likely found himself a feast for the creature that she spoke of.

"How is your powder coming along? Is there anything I can do to help?"

"Nay, I will be quite all right. I can keep watch whilst I work if you want to rest."

Vorax turned her head to the side and listened intently. "Someone is there."

The snapping of a stick caused her to reach for the great axe on her back.

"What is it?" Morvin asked.

An arrow flew past, Vorax turning her shoulder just in time as the arrow deflected from her pauldron.

"Bandits!" she roared, pulling her axe from its harness.

Morvin froze with fear as Vorax sped past him towards two figures that emerged from the trees. The scrawny one on the left was wearing a bandana and held a dagger in each hand. The balding one on the right was thicker-set and wielding a spear.

They were taken by surprise by the advancing Vorax, who took mere seconds to kill the two of them, driving her axe across the stomach of the larger man before slamming her blade into the chest of the scrawny one. The force took him off his feet and he gargled his last breaths as she pinned him to the earth. Two more arrows fired from the trees, one of which bedded into Vorax's shoulder. She growled with rage as she pulled the arrow out, screaming into the darkness.

"Show yourselves, you fucking cowards!" she cried.

A group of five stepped from the shadows, a mixture of men and women sporting hatchets, swords, and axes.

In the moonlight, Morvin could see the golden emblems on their chests.

"These are not bandits!" he yelled. "They are the King's Guard!"

Vorax roared even louder as the group of guards sought to surround them. Movement to the right caught Morvin's attention and he turned to see another group of five guards flanking them. Ahead of him, the sound of growls and groans started as Vorax's metal clashed with theirs. Morvin instinctively reached for his hammer and readied himself for the group that was charging towards him. He was not a fighter, but that did not mean he could not fight, and he felt thankful for the time he had spent with his wife and son when they were practicing their war hammer skills. True, the weapon in his hands was like a toothpick in comparison to a true war hammer, but he was confident that he could give as good as he would get.

With his own battle cry, Morvin ran towards the guards, one of which was a good few feet ahead of the others. He looked younger and less experienced. His mistake.

Morvin gripped his hammer tightly as he slammed it into the young man's knee. With a sickening thud, the guard howled as he bowled over on the ground, his knee shattered. As he hit the ground, Morvin spun and brought down the hammer on his head, then again and again. By the time he regained composure and turned to face the other guards, they were already upon him. Two flanked him, one from his right, one from the left, while a third charged from straight ahead of him and a fourth not far behind. Morvin braced himself; four against one were not odds that he would back himself against. He brought his hammer back behind him, ready to strike in self-defence.

With a thud, a dagger bedded into the chest of one of the bigger guards on his right, her scream of pain short lived before she took her final breath. What followed was fast movement ahead of him and Morvin caught the tail end of a black cloak before another of the guards cried out in pain and collapsed on the ground. There were only two left in this group now, and the one ahead of him found himself coming face-to-face with Skyrar, who moved through the shadows with speed Morvin had never seen before.

The two of them began exchanging blows as the remaining guard, a stocky male, bundled towards Morvin.

Morvin knew that his small Dwarvish frame was deceiving, and he braced himself for the impact from the guard who bore a great axe in his hands. As the man drew close, he raised his axe high. Seizing the opportunity, Morvin barged his shoulder into the stomach of the remaining guard, knocking him sideways. The guard lost his footing and fell to the floor, dropping his axe. Morvin dived on top of him and rained down blows with his hammer over and over until all that remained was a bloody pool of pulp and blood, his own face drawing warmth as it splashed over him.

Vorax continued to clash with four more guards. She was parrying their strikes as they sought to find a way to break her defensive stance.

"Vorax!" Morvin called as he charged towards her to lend her his aid.

Over his shoulder, a bolt of light shot passed him like forked lightning. The blast of energy struck one of the guards and sent her crumpling to the ground where she began to violently convulse. Vorax wasted no time bringing her blade down on her. Only three remained now.

Morvin looked over his shoulder to see where the lightning had come from. Tarin was bracing himself against a cracked tree with one hand outstretched, a pained grimace evident on his face.

"Flank them!" he bellowed.

The three guards stood in front of Vorax, nervously looking at one another for who should strike the enraged, hulking Elf. Taking Tarin's advice, Morvin raced to the left-hand side, drawing the attention of the guard there. Opposite him, Skyrar rose from the shadows, a dagger in each of her hands. The guard in front of her had no time to react as she raised both daggers quickly and buried them into each shoulder. With a crunch, she twisted the blades as the guard screamed out in pain. Morvin stood his ground in a standoff with the attacker in front of him, as neither committed to striking first. Then an arrow slammed into the guard, knocking him over. Morvin turned to see Darmour holding a crossbow, his one good eye pressed against the sight.

The remaining guard stood firm for a matter of seconds, weighing his chances of survival. Then he dropped his sword, turned, and bolted into the darkness.

His steps were short lived as the sound of metal piercing flesh was followed by the gargled breath of the guard. He stepped backwards into the moonlight and Morvin saw a cutlass buried deep into his stomach. As he staggered backwards, another form stepped out from the darkness.

Ulrik's expression was unforgiving as he launched his boot into the hilt of his sword, forcing it deep enough until it reached the man's stomach. The guard dropped to the ground and Ulrik stepped forward to retrieve his blade.

"Well, I have waited a while for some bloodshed," Ulrik said.

When he grinned, Morvin could see nothing but malice in his eyes.

6

"I thought you said this camp was safe!" Morvin asked, his voice raised. This was not what he had expected tonight.

"The King's Guard have clearly been tracking us, most likely because of how we left things in Noren," Tarin answered. He bore the look of someone pleased with the situation, not of concern, which brought alarm to Morvin. "They must have followed us down the mountains and into the woodlands."

"Either way, how do we know there are not more of those fuckers out there?" Morvin asked, pointing into the trees. Dawn was breaking with light lifting over their camp. The songs of the birds rang out, giving a tranquil feeling to the landscape despite there being twelve bodies scattered around the camp. Morvin had not been with the group long and had already started adding to his body count. Whether they deserved it or not, it left a bitter, sinking feeling in the pits of his stomach. He could only hope that it would get easier, that the burden of forcing someone to draw their last breath became less heavy.

"If there were more, they would have shown themselves by now," Tarin said.

"Let them come, I say," said Skyrar.

Vorax growled with pain as Zerina lifted her pauldron from her shoulder, revealing a bloodied wound. She tossed the dirty armour on the ground and placed both her hands over the hole in Vorax's flesh made by the arrow.

"You should have allowed me to heal this immediately, Vorax," Zerina scolded. "You have lost a lot of blood."

Morvin watched with fascination as light emitted from under Zerina's hands while she concentrated.

"Next time, don't rip the arrow from your shoulder. You have made it worse. I may be able to heal some wounds, but I cannot bring you back from the dead."

"Don't we know it," Ulrik growled from the far side of the fire. "When you're all done, I suggest we set our plan into motion and make way to my ship. Our position here is compromised." With that, Ulrik turned and headed off away from the group. Darmour gave Zerina an exasperated look, then followed Ulrik.

Zerina shook her head at Ulrik before returning her attention on Vorax's wound.

"You shouldn't let him talk to you like that," Vorax said.

"I am used to it. It used to bother me, but it doesn't anymore." Zerina raised her hands from the wound to reveal a scar in its place, which left Morvin speechless. "There you go. I would suggest heading to the river to clean up." She reached for a small flask tucked into her belt and uncorked it before taking a drink.

"Thank you, Zerina." Vorax picked up her pauldron from the ground and walked away, rubbing her shoulder where the new scar had formed.

"Please take the Dwarf with you," Skyrar called. "Now

that he is covered in blood, he might be motivated to wash."

Morvin scowled at Skyrar before shrugging his shoulders in agreement.

Vorax chuckled. "Come, the river is this way."

He set off to follow her but quickly stopped, looking at Tarin. "The powder, it is not finished."

"It can wait," Tarin said, giving a nonchalant wave of his hand. The movement caused him to wince with pain, and he massaged the palm and fingers on the hand he had used to cast his magic. "Although I hate to admit it, Ulrik is right. Our camp is now vulnerable, and we do not know if there are more guards out there. You will have to continue with your powder on *Esara's Revenge*, Morvin, despite the risk."

To Morvin's surprise, Tarin was smiling.

"What is it that has you in such a good mood?" he asked. Personally, Morvin did not like the idea of working with such delicate ingredients out on the open seas, but he knew it was only a matter of time before more guards arrived. That was the only thing he was certain of.

"This group, the way we were able to defend camp with our combined skills. It tells me we are ready for the next step in our quest. That we have recruited the right people," Tarin replied gleefully.

"That remains to be seen," Skyrar said.

"Are you coming, Morvin?" Vorax called, her voice stirring the birds in the trees, some which took flight.

"Aye, lass, give me a chance." Morvin rolled his eyes. "Are Elves always this impatient?"

"I would say they are efficient," said Tarin with a grin.

Morvin followed Vorax but was unable to keep up with

her giant stride compared to his own. Before long, they reached the river that ran down via an unknown source which Morvin assumed was the mountains they had passed the day before. It was strangely serene, given that both Morvin and Vorax were covered in blood. The river passed gently through a crack in the ground, the waters running completely clear. Morvin could see fish swimming down its soft current. The trees remained thin but there were some large boulders that gave a decent amount of cover.

"Do these waters run from the corrupted loch you spoke of?" Morvin asked.

"From Loch Bragoa? They do, yes."

"And are these waters not corrupted then?" Morvin asked, concerned for what the waters could do to his skin or even worse, his beard. "I've been growing this thing for eighty-five years, don't want it to be damaged by some strange waters."

Vorax laughed and patted Morvin on the shoulder. "My friend, we have been using these waters for nearly a year as we prepared for this voyage. I can assure you they are not corrupted. I can only assume that the corruption takes place only in the loch itself."

Vorax began removing her armour, leaving it in a pile on the ground. When she removed her chest plate, she revealed a dark-green tunic underneath. Although it was bloodstained, Morvin could still make out the emblem of a tree.

"Don't you know it's rude to stare?"

Morvin averted his gaze straight away. "I'm sorry, I did not mean to, I was simply looking at your emblem."

"Relax, Morvin, I only joke with you." Vorax removed her tunic, unfazed by the presence of the Dwarf. Morvin chose to turn away as he undressed, and he heard Vorax splash into the water, giving a loud whoop.

"Strength, brains, and a sense of humour. Are you sure you're not from Dwarven lineage?" Morvin laughed. "You would make a fine wife. Us Dwarves are in awe of women who can battle." It had been only part of why he had fallen madly in love with Herelda, all those years ago.

"I am afraid you are not my type," Vorax said, grinning as she dipped her hair back into the water.

"Think Dwarves and Elves are races best left unmixed, do you?" Morvin laughed. He knew full well that Dwarves did not seek to breed with anyone other than their own kind.

"Oh gods, no, I am quite open-minded about who I lay with. I have already bedded a Dwarf before." She paused for a moment, thinking. "Or was she a Gnome?"

"You cheeky bastard! Dwarves are nothing like gnomes."

"Are you going to stand by the river all day, or do you intend to bathe?" Vorax said, then plunged her head under the water, disappearing from sight.

Morvin could not remember the last time he had bathed, let alone had the opportunity to go for a swim. He ran towards the water and tucked himself into a ball before dropping into the river. He called out with the glee of a child as a pool of water splashed up around him.

"Oh shit!" he spluttered as he emerged. "It's so fucking cold!" The water was clear and crisp, and with it brought a freshness, as if he bathed in ice brought down from Garuvia. Panicking, he kicked out wildly as his body went into shock from the cold.

Vorax set about laughing. "What did you expect? The water runs from the mountains." She swam towards

Morvin who splashed around in the water like an untrained babe.

Dwarves had less buoyancy in the water than other races, meaning he had to kick his legs harder just to maintain afloat. He bobbed up and down, only just able to tread water. Through some quick, shortened breaths, he acclimatised himself to the jarring temperature.

"You're all right, you," Morvin said. "For an Elf, anyway."

"As are you, Morvin." Vorax paused again. "For a Gnome."

"Ya cheeky shit!" Morvin laughed as he splashed water over the Elven warrior. He could not help but feel that he had made a new friend in Vorax, today, one that he had not expected.

The two of them spent the next hour washing and laughing in the water, giving Morvin a happiness that he had not experienced in a long time.

7

"My lord, our scouts tell us that the Zarubians are on the back foot. If we continue to take the lands to the east of Ashula, we may be able to tip the tide of this war." The general stood proudly, holding his black helmet under his arm. He wore his mail armour when in camp, only wearing his full suit of armour when there was need for battle. One hand was placed behind his back whilst he addressed King Athos Almerion.

King Athos sat at a large beech table. A large map was laid out over the top of it, depicting lands with various markers and figures. His mood was not the best. He was tired of being detained in this keep, even if it had been set up like a fortress for his own safety.

"General Precian, we have been here before. We have been here many a time before. How many times have I been told that if we take these lands or that land, it will tip the tides of war in our favour? I grow tired of your empty words." King Athos raised his head impatiently as his attention was brought away from the battle map. "Have we not been here in this very keep for six months now? Pushed back, forced to defend ourselves."

"True, the Zarubians have proven more skilled than we realised, especially with their use of magic."

"Something your scouts failed to warn us of before we invaded these lands. It near crippled us, wiping out scores of our troops and putting us onto uneven footing." King Athos spoke firmly, clearly indicating his displeasure with his general's interruption. "If not for Morgana's efforts in Levanthria, we would have fallen before now. It is thanks to her advancement of magic that we have been able to fight back."

General Precian did not appear happy with this, and King Athos noticed his clenched jaw. "My lord, I only asked for caution when dabbling in magic. It had been outlawed for so long, we still do not know the full capabilities of the power. It is dangerous."

"I don't seem to recall you complaining when Morgana's mages prevented our battalion at Gregenhime from falling. When it was your life spared," Athos spat. "I refuse to stay in this keep any longer. It is abhorrent that we have become so stationary."

"We merely wait for reinforcements, my lord. When these arrive, we will have the forces here to advance into Ashula and leave this place. I feel if we can take these lands" – General Precian pointed a heavy finger to a plot of barren land on the war map – "then we can spread our forces here." He pointed at another space on the map. "Once in place, we will be in the perfect position to take the capital. Zarubia will be ours and this war will be ended."

"Is there anything else?" Athos growled.

"There is, my lord. I have received word from Levan-thria. The kingdom of Eltera has fallen from the rule of Lord

Wistler. An organised group of thieves and scoundrels have taken control of the kingdom." The general swallowed nervously. "This means the weapon and armour supply produced by their forge has stopped entirely."

King Athos pushed his chair back and stood up, placing his hands in the small of his back as he moved in front of the general. He leant into his ear and hissed, "Know this, General. Should your scouts misinform us again, should this battle plan of yours fail, then I will see to it that you are executed for treason and Levanthria informed of your incompetence. Your lands will be stripped and any family that bear your name exiled. That is, if I do not slaughter them myself. Do you understand?" He spoke through gritted teeth, spittle leaving his mouth. "As for Eltera, I will deal with whatever is going on there."

"Yes, my lord." General Precian nodded, turning away as his cheeks reddened, either from anger or fear, Athos was not sure. He did not care either way.

As General Precian left the room, Athos took out some parchment and laid it over the battle table. He dipped a quill in ink and began to scribe an urgent correspondence.

Morgana,

I have received a report regarding the condition of Eltera following the witch trials. It causes me great concern to learn that after three years, Lord Wistler is unable to bring order about the people to ensure taxes are collected in a timely manner. With my forces stretched thin, we need all available resources if we are to finally end this war and claim these lands as our own. The spellcasters you trained have proven most helpful, but as you warned, their continued magic use takes a toll on their bodies, rendering them useless. For this reason, I request that you continue your experiments around magic and continue to train those that are able to wield magic so that they can aid us.

I do have one further request of you. If you can fulfil it, it will certainly put you in my favour when I return. As Codrin currently stands as ward over Askela, I need you to go to Eltera. I need you to find out why Lord Wistler is unable to get control of his people and ensure that coin and weapons are being provided for our forces. Their forge is renowned for producing the strongest armour in Levanthria and it is imperative that we regain use of it. Head to Eltera, take back control, and help me end this war against the Zarubians. Because Eltera is the nearest city to the southern ports, I fear that foreign forces such as the Barbaraqs may seek to take advantage of my absence. Eltera cannot fall. Levanthria's fate may depend upon it.

I will make this more than worth your while when I return. After all, a king needs a queen.

Kindest regards,
King Athos Almerion

The king threw his quill to the side and slammed a clenched fist onto the table, knocking over the markers that sat strategically across the map, then raised his hands to massage his temple. He dreaded to think what he might return to in Levanthria if Morgana and Codrin failed to maintain stability. His cousin Jareb had fallen, leaving Athos the last of their family line. Maybe it was time for him to finally return and settle down to produce an heir for the crown. With the magical prowess that Morgana wielded, perhaps she was exactly who he needed to secure a new bloodline under the Almerion name, one that would have magic flowing through its veins.

"Krooshan!" the king shouted.

A young soldier in mail armour arrived within moments from outside the war room. He had a nervous air about him as he stood before the king, which made Athos feel exasperated.

"Yes, sire?" he said, his voice cracking with nerves as he spoke.

"I have an important task of you, boy." Athos blew on the letter before testing the ink was dry. Once satisfied, he sealed it with wax and pressed his signet ring into it. "See to it that this letter goes straight to Askela and into Morgana's hands. It needs to get to her as fast as possible. Can you make this happen?" He raised his hand nonchalantly, the letter sitting between two of his fingers.

"Yes, my lord, I will see to it myself." The boy took the letter from the king and stood to attention, awaiting further command.

"Well, what are you waiting for? Get out!" Athos barked.

"Right away, sir!" The boy scurried out of the chamber to deliver Morgana's letter.

Athos was tired of being surrounded by incompetent fools. It was time to regain their advantage in this war, no matter whose lives it may cost.

8

By the time the group had bathed and headed to *Esara's Revenge*, it was already the middle of the afternoon. The ship had been berthed in a small cove just beyond the woodlands. Morvin sat in the back of the cart, his barrel of powder on one side of him, the wooden box of ingredients on the other.

He smiled as he took in a breath of the woodlands for one last time as they headed over a rocky path. Beneath them sat a picturesque cove, complete with a stony, pebbled beach. The surrounding rock faces offered perfect protection, and Morvin felt strangely calm. He had never set sail on a boat, but he looked forward to experiencing it for the first time. This whole quest so far had already been a bit of an adventure for him, pushing him outside of the comfort zone of his home. Herelda would be so proud of him. His boy, too. They had pushed him for so long to travel away from the mining town where he had always lived, but he had always been too stubborn to agree to it. His wife had seen more of the world through battle than he could ever imagine. Feeling proud of himself, Morvin searched the sky above and smiled as he thought of his wife. He took some comfort in the possibility that Herelda was watching over him. The clouds were calm and unmoving, the breeze gentle and reassuring. The only thing over which he held a semblance of anxiety was the potential sea sickness that Skyrar had been teasing him about all day.

When they arrived at the cove, Tarin pulled the horses to stop and climbed down to untether them from their bindings. He gave each a scratch behind their rears before they both bucked and ran off down the pebbled beach.

The two grey horses danced around each other, jumping into one another as though playing for the first time. Morvin watched, thankful for the freedom Tarin had bestowed on them. The hair of their manes flowed behind them as they pranced around, sand and dust spraying up in the air.

Morvin could not help but feel that having a wash in the river had put him in good spirits. His mind felt less clouded, his eyes did not bear their usual heaviness, and the odour that usually clung to him was no more.

He had fetched some finer clothes from his effects and ditched his filthy, blood-soaked garments by the river. Vorax had joked with him that she was surprised his old clothes had not crawled off themselves whilst they bathed.

In fact, one could have been forgiven for not recognising Morvin, for not only was he wearing fine, navy-blue robes, but Vorax had even helped him get his beard in order. He looked down upon himself and ran his hand through his thick, now-plaited beard. It was something his wife once did for him on a regular basis, something he had neglected since her passing.

As the rest of the group set about loading the items onto

the ship, Vorax pulled open the back of the cart and gave Morvin a kind smile. "Pass me the barrel," she asked.

Morvin picked up the weighty, wooden barrel and staggered towards her, his legs straddling either side of it as he walked. Vorax scooped it up under one arm and laughed before carrying it off to the ship. Morvin hopped off the back of the cart, picked up the wooden box, then turned to take in the large boat that sat within the cove.

The main sail of *Esara's Revenge* bore the emblem of three skulls, each with a blade travelling through it. One from the left, one from above, and one from the opposite side. Underneath, larger grey sails were already extended, with various ropes and netting holding everything into shape. The sea breeze had not yet taken hold of them, allowing them to sag slightly.

The boat itself was impressive. Morvin had seen boats at nearby docks in Lorean, but none as dark or as gothic as this. The wood was stained almost black, the railings intricate and curling like multiple pieces of wood had been intertwined around one another and stained slightly different dark shades. At the head of the ship was a carving of what appeared to be a young girl. Her hair had been carved to look as though the wind blew it back, her face frozen in a fierce battle cry. Not something one would usually associate with a child, Morvin thought.

Morvin climbed into the small boat at the edge of the beach, his wooden box under one arm. Vorax, Skyrar, and Tarin were already sat inside waiting for him. Skyrar laughed as Morvin almost lost his footing when the boat rocked with his added weight. He was just about able to keep composure before sitting down, and Vorax, already holding both oars, set about rowing them to the ship.

Morvin was the last to climb aboard, following the last

of their supplies being winched up onto the deck. He looked up at the side of the ship's hull, which looked like a colossus, reminding him just how small he was. But beyond it, the open ocean reminded him how small the ship was in comparison.

He climbed up the rickety rungs of the rope ladder which clung to the side. The ship groaned under the strain of its anchor, ready to set sail, and Morvin wondered for a moment if Skyrar would want the ship to move whilst he was in this vulnerable position just to entertain her.

When he reached the top, Morvin inelegantly rolled over the railing, landing on his side before quickly climbing back to his feet. He hoped that no one saw his entrance, but when he raised his head, Skyrar was grinning at him. He responded with a crude hand gesture, which she returned.

She turned away to join Vorax and Darmour, who were already setting up position at a circular wheel at the centre of the ship, and Morvin followed close behind. Zerina, Ulrik, and Tarin were in conversation at the helm, peering over a large map in Ulrik's hands.

"Well, look at you," Darmour said, beaming. "Tarin! Who is this finely dressed Dwarf you have brought aboard, and what have you done with Morvin?" He gestured for Morvin to join him. "Come, friend, we will need your strength in raising this anchor. Although I would like to see if Vorax could raise it by herself."

Morvin took up position as requested, grabbing hold of the large wheel.

"Ready!" Darmour shouted.

"Raise the anchor!" Ulrik called back in a deep, growling voice. Zerina took the map from him and headed down the ornate carved steps, the craftmanship of which Morvin could truly appreciate.

As Morvin pressed against the wheel, he was met by a great resistance. He used the power not just from his legs but from his arms in tandem with the others. The wheel began to turn slowly, and between the four of them, they continued to heave until the anchor was raised. In an instant, the ship drifted, either pulled by the currents of the water or the wind that caught the sails above. It was a strange sensation as the boat rocked, and for a moment, Morvin felt witless as he shifted his feet over the moving floor.

"Have you ever sailed before?" Darmour asked.

"First time," he answered as he straightened up his robe.

"Know this: As long as you respect the ocean, she will respect you in return. She can be as serine and calm as the gentle waters of a lake, but she can soon turn the tides of these waters into a furious, vengeful grave for those who are not prepared."

Morvin's eyes widened, but Darmour broke into a wide smile. "Luckily for you, you sail with three notorious pirates who have traversed the most dangerous parts of these waters. Where we sail, the waters should be calm."

"How long will it take to get to Zarubia?" Morvin asked.

"By my reckoning, with a good wind on our side, about seven or eight days," Darmour said whilst tying the thick rope around a metal knot on the floor.

As the ship left the cove, Morvin took in the spectacular view behind them. For the first time in his life, he was not on the lands of Levanthria, and his heart skipped as the realisation dawned on him. The rocky mountains, the cove, the woodlands just beyond it made such a beautiful sight. It was a far cry from the industrial town where Morvin had spent his sheltered life for the last hundred years or so.

Beyond a gap in the trees, Morvin saw the two recently freed horses standing side by side as if they were waving them goodbye. He took in another deep breath, savouring every moment as woodland air was replaced with that of a crisp, salty tinge.

"Where did you put the barrel?" Morvin asked Vorax.

"It's belowdecks. If you drop below the crew's quarters, you will see a workstation you should be able to put to good use."

"Aye, providing the waters stay kind," Morvin added. "No time like the present." He had just over a week to continue to make the powder, and he was hoping he would also have time to tinker with the new boom pistol he had started crafting.

He headed to the crew's quarters in the bottom of the ship where beds were fashioned from hammocks suspended between various posts. As intricate and impressive as the main deck of the ship had looked, this was the opposite. It was dark and dank with a smell of damp mixed with salt water and sweat. Even by Morvin's boldly low standards of odour, it caused his nose to twinge, and he felt himself gag slightly. Or was that the effects of sea sickness? A strange knot had begun forming in his stomach which he was unfamiliar with as the boat rocked and groaned.

He made his way down another flight of steps and found a large wooden table illuminated in a white, starlight glow caused by the powder he had already mixed earlier. The table was huge, so he manoeuvred another nearby barrel in front of it to stand on as a stool.

His vials and bottles of ingredients were soon lined up and a pile of ironite ore sat by the side of a large metal anvil on which a bloodied hammer sat.

It was going to be a long week of physical labour, but

Morvin cricked his neck and rolled up his sleeves before setting to work. He had a task to complete and a contraption to finish building. Hard work was not something he was afraid of, but there was a different pressure on him now. The fates of everyone on this ship relied on his success. As a tinkerer and an inventor, Morvin was used to failure. It was how he learned. But now, amongst these men and women, failure was not an option. It was a pressure that was foreign to him, one that if he did not keep a grip of, risked drowning him. Knowing he needed to get started on the task he was brought here to do, Movin lifted a piece of the ironite onto the anvil, took hold of the bloodied hammer, and set to work.

9

The crescent moon reflected in the calm waters of the ocean as *Esara's Revenge* gently rocked back and forth.

Morvin had retreated to the main deck to get some fresh air. It was the dead of night and most of the group were sleeping, either in the crew's chambers or the captain's quarters.

Wind tossed his hair back and ruffled the frayed edges of his thick beard. He savoured the moment. As usual, Morvin had been so absorbed in his task that hours had passed. He had ground most of the ironite up but his arms and shoulders ached. He did not know how much time had passed, such was the nature of his focus. His face was blackened from dust sticking to his sweat-laden face.

The sound of waves breaking could be heard, but peering into the distance, Morvin could see nothing but darkness ahead of the ship. He knew they were moving; the ship's swaying told him that much. Another knot in his stomach lurched but it was a feeling he was becoming accustomed to now. Behind him at the helm of the ship

72

stood a fatigued Darmour, his one good eye alternating from looking ahead of him to searching the stars, to checking the compass in his hand and tweaking the wheel in his other hand.

It was something that fascinated Morvin, being able to charter a course with nothing but the stars and a compass to go on. He could not quite get his head around how one would come to learn this, for stars changed and moved depending on the seasons.

The sound of someone violently throwing up interrupted the tranquillity of the night.

When Morvin realised that the source of the noise was coming from an unkempt Skyrar, his grin could have rivalled the crescent moon above if it were turned sideways.

She was leant over the side of the boat as she emptied her guts. Sensing too good of an opportunity, Morvin walked across to her and patted her on the back. "Feeling a little seasick, are we?" He beamed at her. Skyrar had taken great pleasure in teasing him about riding on a boat for the first time and goading him about sea sickness. And now here she was.

A gargled noise rose from inside her and she attempted to vomit once more. Nothing other than a violent retch left her lips, however, as she heaved to no avail.

"Fuck off!" she said, turning to reveal sunken, bloodshot eyes. Her skin was even paler than usual, and messy hair stuck to her face.

"Well, aren't you a picture to behold," Morvin laughed, exchanging a playful glance with Darmour who seemed to find the whole thing entertaining himself.

"Haven't you got powder to make? I am in no need of being tormented by you." She stuttered towards the end of her sentence before turning and heaving over the side of the ship again.

Morvin let out a laugh, his hands clapping against his stomach. He knew Skyrar would be gloating over him if their positions were reversed. That said, he did want to check she was okay. He placed his hand gently on her back and rubbed it before patting her lightly.

"Better out than in, lass, especially if you're feeling sick. In my experience, there is no point trying to fight it." Under his palm, he felt Skyrar's muscles twitch and convulse as another wave of sickness came over her. "There, there, try this." He reached into his tunic and retrieved a little bottle of black liquid. "Made it as soon as we were on board. It's my mother's recipe. Always helped with my boy when he was younger whenever sickness took him. It might help settle your stomach."

A desperate Skyrar turned and snatched at the bottle, raising it towards the moon to examine it. The black liquid had the consistency of treacle.

She furrowed her brows. "What's in it?"

"Charcoal, honey, turmeric, and a few other bits. Trust me, it should settle your stomach. Won't do much for your smile for a few hours, but we don't have that to worry about with you anyway."

Skyrar uncorked the vial and took a swig of the liquid, halving it in one.

"Easy, now. You will be shitting like a veroga for the rest of this journey if you drink too much."

Skyrar grimaced at first but came to tilt her head as she shuddered. "Eurgh," she said. "That is such a strange flavour. Tastes grainy, too."

"Aye, the charcoal makes it so."

"Will it help with the spins? Honestly, that's the worst part. I feel like my head is in the midst of a tornado."

"Unfortunately not," Morvin said, rubbing her back once more and walking beside her as they made their way towards the steps down to the crew's chambers. "If you find the nausea coming back, take another swig of that tonic and it should see you right by the morning."

"Thank you," Skyrar said. She gave him a strange look, as if uncertain whether to trust his kindness.

"I had a wife and a son," Morvin said suddenly, surprising himself. "Herelda was my wife's name. The strongest and bravest Dwarf that I have ever known. We built our house together, took us three years." He cast his eyes out at the blackened void they sailed though, reliving the memories of the life they had shared, of the life they wanted to build together. "She was strong-minded, too, quite like you."

He paused, taking in a breath of the fresh sea air as Skyrar watched him in silence. "We were happy with the life we built. Her father was one of the foremen at the mines at Kragoa, and let me tell you, the things that Dwarf made me do in order to gain her hand." He laughed to himself. To go back to that time would be all he could ever dream of.

"I tell you, in the end it was only because he loved his daughter as fiercely as I did, and that she told him she was going to marry me either way, that he accepted. And for forty-seven short years, we built everything we had. Grew the little plot of trees where I found you two prying. The best part is, we were happy. I was as happy as I thought that I could ever be. I had everything I wanted. A job in the quarry, a beautiful wife, Herelda." Morvin's eyes grew wide as he spoke of his past. "Then we were blessed with some-thing we thought would never happen to us, after years of trying, and boy did we try." A wry grin flared in the corner of his mouth.

Skyrar shuddered, apparently repulsed by the thought, but she seemed to be intently listening. Morvin had not spoken of his family in years, and now that he had started, he could not stop.

"We named him Korvin, and I had never known love like it. You are told when you are growing up of how it feels, but to experience it, to hold a smaller version of yourself in your hands . . ."

"I never experienced it," Skyrar said, her tone softer than what Morvin was used to. "The love of a parent."

"He gave us purpose, and for the next forty years, I watched him grow. We watched him form his first beard, his first plait, make his first hammer in the forges of the Kragoan Mountains. We saw him grow into a skilled fighter just like his ma, all while I continued to work in the quarry whilst tinkering in the basement. I was not the fighter, that I left to Herelda."

Morvin found himself choking on his words as a heavy lump formed in his throat. "You spend all your life knowing that you have plenty of time with those that you love. I am only considered middle aged, even at one hundred and thirteen years old. We had so much time left together. Then the king announced he was going to war with the Zarubians, and able fighters were to put themselves forward for conscription. As proud Dwarves, my wife and son bravely put themselves forward without hesitation."

Morvin's cheeks felt a fresh blast of cold as tears ran down his face, leaving clean tracks in his grubby skin. "I would never have stopped them from going. It is considered a great honour to fight in battle. My wife had many a token braided into her hair from the battles she had won over the years. Herelda Steelhammer. I knew that war had risks, but my wife and son were skilled with their hammers, and I knew that they would return."

Morvin sniffed up his tears, pausing for a moment as the memories became too tough to bear. "They should have returned. Three years ago, I received word that both of them had fallen in the Battle of Red Cragg."

Skyrar's eyes flickered with recognition. "I am sorry, Morvin."

It was a notorious battle that many were familiar with, for those that were sent to fight were said to have been sacrificed tactically by King Athos Almerion.

"You won't need me to explain that it was a tactical move that would bring about thousands of Levanthrian deaths, but left the Zarubians open to be flanked. A move that the king later decided against, after he had already sent his soldiers away. It was too late to call them back."

Morvin closed his eyes tightly. What he would do to see them one last time, to tell them how much he loved them. Something that he would never be able to do.

His tone turned to one of anger and vitriol. "Their lives meant nothing to the bastard king. But they meant everything to me." He raised his head, his eyes meeting Skyrar's. "This is why I am here. This is why I want to help. In my wife's and son's names, I vow to do what I can to make sure we succeed. That we assassinate the king."

"I can't begin to imagine what you must have gone through."

"I know you don't trust me, that you think I am a liability because I am not a fighter like you. But I assure you, I have the fiercest of fires burning deep within my belly."

Skyrar stared at Morvin blankly. For a moment he thought she might mock him for sharing his tale. Instead, she said in a low voice, "I have spent most of my life on the streets. My parents were taken to the dungeons in Askela when they could not afford to pay taxes to Lord Jareb, taxes that Morgana and Codrin enforced." Her cheeks reddened. "I never saw them again."

Morvin was not sure what to say.

She made to leave, but stopped in her tracks to peer over her shoulder. "I'm saying we might have more in common than I thought." Then she made her way down the stairs into the darkness that the chambers offered.

For a while, Morvin stood there deep in thought. Finally, he walked slowly down the steps, deciding that the powder could wait. He needed rest. When he entered the crew's quarters, Tarin's snoring was louder than one of Morvin's hammer blows.

Morvin still had not got used to the hammock, and he was grateful that everyone else was already asleep as he awkwardly climbed in. The fabric strained under his weight and Morvin worried that it would give way and tear, sending him crashing to the floor and waking everyone up. Instead, Morvin lay his head back and stared at the dark boards above him, letting out a sigh.

This was the first time he had truly stopped to think about what he was doing. Just a few weeks ago he had been home, tinkering with his boom pistol and experimenting with powder. Now he found himself aboard a feared pirate ship with what could only be described as a strange group of individuals at best.

Had he been naive? He banished the thought. For the first time in too long, there was a rekindled fire in his belly that could rival brimstone. He had a purpose, a reason for being here.

As Morvin tried to sleep, the boat rocked and swayed,

and a wave of nausea crept up on him. He fought it off, and focused on Herelda and Korvin, wishing he had not given his entire vial of remedy to Skyrar.

"Good night, my love," Morvin murmured. What he would give to have just one more day with them. This was the reason he was doing all this, this was why he was willing to travel so far, to endure this sickness. It would all be worthwhile in the end.

IO

Morvin awoke to his stomach growling louder than a dragon's roar. At first he was unsure if this was because he was going to be sick or because he was ravenous. His beard was damp from drool, and he brought his sleeve up to mop up what he could. His eyes were heavy, and he let out a wide yawn before smacking his lips together. Then an alluring fragrance smacked him in the face.

For a moment he forgot he was in a hammock. As he tried to sit up, it spun on its side, flinging him to the floor with a thud.

"Blasts!" he cursed.

"Finally awake," Skyrar said. She was sitting on a barrel in the corner of the room.

"Were you watching me whilst I slept, lass?" Morvin laughed.

"Don't flatter yourself." She smiled. "We've been taking bets on how long you would sleep for. I must admit, I didn't think it was possible. I've been sat here for hours flicking peragu seeds at you and you haven't so much as flinched."

She flicked another hardened seed at Morvin, which bounced off his forehead and landed in a pile of others that lay scattered around his upturned hammock.

"Turns out, Tarin was right. The best way to a sleeping Dwarf is through his belly. He had Darmour cook some fresh fish for us for dinner."

Morvin dusted himself down and flicked some of the seeds from him that had clung to his tunic. "Dinner? How long have I been asleep?"

"Three bloody days."

"Shit!" It had been a long time since Morvin had slept so long and peacefully.

"We wanted to wake you, but Tarin insisted on letting you rest. I knew Dwarves could sleep well, but I didn't realise how much!"

"We Dwarves don't need to sleep as often, but three days is a lot longer than usual," he admitted. Maybe it was because of the seasickness, maybe it was the unburdening of his story about Herelda and Korvin. Whatever the reason, that was three days gone that he could have spent making powder. The urge to get to work straight away took hold of him, but his stomach growled even louder, reminding him that he needed to eat.

Feeling fresher than a forty-year-old Dwarf, Morvin skipped up the stairs, his mind less clouded with darkened thoughts. As the harsh light of the day greeted him, his eyes stung and he raised a hand to offer some shielding. The warmth in the air was intense, like nothing he had experienced. For a moment he wondered if he had inadvertently stepped into a furnace.

Ulrik was at the helm of the ship, an angry gaze on the horizon as if the waves had somehow offended him. He still wore his long, full-body cloak despite the heat. Everyone else stood around a small stove upon which four large fish were sizzling away.

"Ah, he rises." Tarin finished chewing on some of the cooked fish and tossed the bones overboard.

"Looks like your plan worked to raise him," Darmour laughed. "I thought you were dead, Dwarf."

"You must have needed the sleep," said Zerina, smiling. She flipped one of the freshly cooked fish onto a small wooden plate and passed it to Morvin.

The fish sounded as though it was still cooking but that did not stop Morvin from picking it up with his fingers and biting into it. He had the table manners of a pig, and the others looked on in fascination as he devoured the fish with incredible speed.

"Does it not burn?" Tarin asked, helping himself to another.

"I've wielded a hammer since I was a babe. I've worked in furnaces and forges for one hundred years. After a while, it thickens the skin."

Birds flew around in circles above, diving into the ocean each time one of them tossed a fish carcass overboard.

"How far off land are we? Morvin asked, letting out a large belch. Now he had a belly full of food, he felt ready to get to work.

"We should hit land in just a few hours. That harshness you feel from the sun, that is a sign that we have reached the desolate lands of Zarubia," said Tarin.

"And what is the plan? Up until now all you have told me is that you want to use my powder, but you have not explained why. If we have nearly hit these shores, would it not be beneficial for you to actually tell us how we are going to assassinate the king?"

Tarin looked out at the ocean and closed his eyes as if

savouring the warmth on his skin. "You are right, it is time. Ulrik, may we use your quarters?"

Ulrik nodded, his focus remaining on steering the ship.

The group followed Tarin into the captain's quarters. Inside, there were two beds, one larger and one smaller. The room was tidy, and red velvet quilts offered more luxury than down in the crew's chambers. A bowl of vibrant green and red apples and a pink jarjoba fruit sat on a large desk at the back of the room.

Morvin's eyes lit up at the sight of the fresh fruit and he pushed past everyone to get to the bowl. "May I?" he asked.

"Help yourself," Zerina answered. "Just don't eat the jarjoba fruit. Ulrik keeps it to remind them of home."

It was the jarjoba fruit Morvin craved the most. The bittersweet taste would have been an explosion in his mouth. Instead, he scooped up one of the red apples and bit into it with an audible crunch. The flavour was intense and helped clear his palate after the smoky fish he had just demolished. Beside the fruit bowl sat a large map, its edges frayed and curling in on itself. A couple of stones, an opal, and a dagger had been used to hold down each corner to keep the map flat.

The map depicted a land that Morvin was not familiar with. Fascinated, he started tracing the lines, the mountains, the rivers, the plains that expanded the world in Morvin's mind. In the top corner of the map, 'Zarubia' was written in bold letters with a compass marking north, east, south, and west. The coastline was on the west, with a circle drawn around a fort labelled 'Kesheria'.

"Gather round, everyone." Tarin placed both hands on the table to look over the map as Skyrar, Zerina, Vorax, and Darmour joined them at the table.

"I appreciate the patience you have all shown over the

last year whilst we readied ourselves for this quest. For months, Ulrik and I have worked on a plan, a way in which we would be able to infiltrate the king's camp, a way to get close to him so we can end his tyrannical reign."

"Get on with it," Skyrar spat. "We all know why we are here."

Tarin rolled his eyes and huffed. Morvin had not known him long but already knew that Tarin was a storyteller. In fact, Morvin often enjoyed the tales of which he spoke.

"Very well," Tarin said. "It has taken a year for us to get to this position that we find ourselves in now, but I was working on this long before then. You see, we are in this position because I have someone on the inside, someone who shares the same hatred for the king as we all do. It is because of this shared goal that we have been summoned as reinforcements for the king's forces, disguised as a band of mercenaries. In just a few hours, we will reach land. From there, we will travel east until we reach Kesheria, where King Athos is holed up."

"Your plan is to have us pose as mercenaries?" Skyrar demanded, clearly unimpressed. "How is that supposed to help us get close to the king? You told us he was paranoid, only sharing an audience with a few. We won't get anywhere near him this way!"

Tarin smiled, undeterred by her uncertainty. "That was why, when I heard of an explosion in Noren, I had to go and see the cause. Find the person who created it." Tarin gave Morvin a nod. "With him and his powder, we won't need to get close to the king."

Morvin was beginning to catch on. "Most of the ironite is ground down now. All that remains is to mix together the ingredients. I am yet to finalise a weapon that is able to harness its power, however. After all, how useful is one of my boom pistols if they can only fire one shot?" Due to the long sleep he had, Morvin had not had any time to work on his attempt at recreating his contraption.

Tarin's smile grew even wilder, a spark igniting in his eyes. "I did not bring you here for your boom pistol, Morvin. We are going to transport as many barrels of that powder of yours as we can underneath Kesheria. We are going to bring that stone fortress crashing down on top of the king. And with it, a new age for Levanthria."

Morvin could not help but feel slightly disappointed.

"What is it?" Tarin asked.

"It's just . . ." Morvin glanced at Skyrar. "After what the king did to me, what he took from me . . . I want my boom pistol to deliver his final moments. He took everything away from me when he sent my wife and son to slaughter."

"This isn't just about your hatred, Morvin," Vorax said. "We all have our reasons for being here."

"If not for the king, my sisters would not have been executed at the witch trials in Eltera," Zerina said, placing a hand on Morvin's shoulder. "And Ulrik would not have walked their darkened path."

"I have had to spend the last ten years looking over my shoulder," Darmour added. "The king has made it near impossible for anyone working at sea to earn a fair living other than if you conscript to his navy. I've been on the run for as long as I can remember. A pirate's harsh life is the only life I know. I have seen too many good men and women fall under the ships bearing the king's colours."

"And I was deemed a traitor for refusing to fight for the king. Hunted because I was born with the ability to wield magic," Tarin finished.

Morvin lifted his head and he knew that his fantasy of

watching the king die by his own hand was selfish. He was not the only one who had been wronged by King Athos.

"Aye, you're right," he said. "I suppose the key thing is that we are successful. That at the end of that darkened day, whenever we get there, we are victorious. Know that I will not stop producing this powder until we are ready. Until I am standing on the smouldering stones of Kesheria. You have my word."

II

M orvin worked continuously for the next few hours making his powder. He found that already having the ironite ore crushed greatly sped up his process, and he managed to fill two barrels. When that was done, he forged four metal shafts and wrapped them in leather, then tinkered with the barrels until the two shafts were firmly attached to each one, curving out from the metal bindings that held the barrels together at the top. Without horses or a cart, they would need to carry the barrels themselves.

Privately, Morvin filled a hardened bottle made from the skin of a gruvebear with the powder and tucked it away inside his tunic for his own purposes.

The sun was high and relentless by the time *Esara's Revenge* made it to the shoreline. The lands of Zarubia were far different than those of Levanthria. The closest thing to it that Morvin could think of were the Biterian Plains, except the climate here was far harsher. He had never seen so much sand stretching out before him.

They made port within a cove that Tarin's informant

had instructed them to find. It consisted of only a narrow opening for them to sail in through very carefully. Here, there were no mountains to keep them hidden; if Zarubian forces were to travel by, the crew would be wide open for an attack, which meant they had little time to dally. Large, jagged rocks protruded from the ocean in an outwards manner as if the land itself had formed defences against invaders.

"These rock formations do not look natural," Tarin mused. "Perhaps the gods themselves carved them."

Morvin followed his gaze towards the spiked rock formations that surrounded *Esara's Revenge* as Darmour steered the ship through. He did not find the sight to be very welcoming.

Once they had managed to get through the opening, they found the cove's waters to be calmer and less rocky. The group quickly set to work on transporting their supplies and Morvin's powder ashore.

By the time they had finished unloading the ship, all of them were dripping with sweat from the harsh sun above them.

"Should it not be nearly nightfall?" a tired Morvin asked. His tunic was soaked with sweat and his mouth was dry. It was heat like this that made him curse his thick beard and long hair. Morvin thought he was well-adjusted to heat, having spent his life working around a forge, but this was something else entirely.

"It only grows dark in these parts in the dead of night," Darmour answered. "Even then it doesn't remain dark for long." He carried one of the oak barrels that contained Morvin's powder and dropped it onto the yellowish-orange sand with a thud.

"Careful!" Morvin warned, his heartbeat rising. "I still don't know how volatile that powder is!"

"Oh, right." Darmour raised his hand to the back of his head awkwardly. "Guess we don't want that exploding on us here."

"Exactly."

"What are these for?" Vorax asked, placing the second barrel carefully onto the sand and inspecting the leather-covered bar that Morvin had attached to it.

"To help us carry them," Morvin answered. "I'll show you. Vorax, if you don't mind helping."

Vorax picked up the barrel and Morvin walked in front of her, stepping backwards until his shoulders hit the bottom of the barrel. "Lower it."

Vorax did as she was asked, and the bars slipped over his shoulders. The weight of the barrel nearly toppled him backwards. It was so large that it nearly covered his entire back. Part of the barrel pressed into his spine uncomfortably, but it would make transporting the powder easier than carrying it in their arms.

"Genius." Tarin clapped, rushing over to examine Morvin's invention. "Wearing a barrel like a sack!"

"It's heavy, but if we alternate between those of us strong enough to carry them, it shouldn't slow us down too much. I may as well carry this one first, given it's already in place."

"I'll carry the other," Vorax offered. Zerina and Darmour helped lift the second barrel onto her back.

"Are you sure you want to be wearing all that armour in this heat?" Darmour asked as the two of them shook the barrel to make sure it was firmly in place. Vorax's shoulder pauldrons ensured that the bars were a snug fit. She stood up with ease, appearing unfazed by the weight.

"It would be a great dishonour to my grandfather if I was to leave it behind on the ship," she said. "This heat is intense, but I am sure we will soon find some shade to rest."

"I wouldn't count on that, Vorax," Darmour said. "Some of the harshest lands I have set foot on, these."

Vorax rolled her eyes in frustration. She was the strongest woman that Morvin had ever laid eyes on, and he knew that she would have the high levels of endurance needed for this next part of their journey.

"I've had enough of all this talk." Ulrik pushed past the group and set off stomping through the sands "We need to move."

"How does he even know if we are going the right way?" Skyrar asked. "There is nothing ahead of us but sand."

"My dear girl, navigating land is not too much different from navigating the ocean," Tarin laughed. "Come, we have much land to cover." He scooped up Morvin's wooden box and followed Ulrik.

"What about the ship?" Morvin asked, looking at Darmour.

"Would take a brave man to try and take *Esara's Revenge*," the pirate said, giving Morvin a toothy grin.

In Morvin's opinion, it was either overconfidence or ignorance that fuelled Darmour, and it felt strange for them to leave the ship unattended. He had not thought of what they would do with it once they arrived, but they could not afford to leave anyone behind. Tarin had made it clear that if they were going to be successful in their quest, they needed all of them.

Ulrik stopped and turned around, staring as *Esara's Revenge* where it bobbed lazily in the cove. Then he raised his hand, motioning towards it. At first Morvin thought he was giving it an odd wave in farewell, but then he realised that Ulrik was channelling his magic. It was the first time Morvin had witnessed it, and it didn't look pleasant.

Thick veins protruded from Ulrik's neck and he grimaced as if holding in a scream of pain. He grunted with the effort, his hands contorting and snapping as he waved them in the direction of *Esara's Revenge*. The ship shook and flickered as though it were a mirage in the desert.

Morvin's jaw dropped as the ship transformed into a jagged rock, blending into those that surrounded it. "That's glamour magic?" he asked.

Zerina placed a delicate hand on Ulrik's shoulder and a gentle glow emanated from underneath it. Ulrik's pained expression subsided, and he let out a sigh of relief as Zerina removed a flask from her satchel and took a sip from it.

"What did you do?" Morvin asked.

"I acted as a siphon. Magic destroys the bodies of those who wield it. I can use my power to make sure that doesn't happen. We have found it also enables the glamour magic to remain, even if Ulrik is not around. Our ship will remain hidden until we return," Zerina said, shaking her hand as if it pained her.

The group was soon underway, and it wasn't long before Morvin's legs were burning deeply. The terrain was hard to navigate due to wading through soft sand. There was no breeze to cool them as they marched across the harsh terrain. His breath was heavy as he focused on keeping up with the others as best he could. His Dwarven frame gave him an increased strength over the others – except for Vorax, whose strength was unrivalled – but his legs were shorter, meaning that for every step the others took, it was two for him.

There was no sign of life around them other than the few birds that circled above. They looked larger than ones

Morvin had seen in Levanthria. Their wings were thicker and darker, and he caught a glimpse of large, dangerous looking talons.

Noticing Morvin looking up at them, Darmour called out, "Those bastards will look to pick off anyone who falls behind. Can't say how long it may have been since they last ate."

Suddenly Morvin felt more motivated to keep up. Digging deep, he picked up the pace and closed the gap between him and the rest of the group.

More time passed. Morvin did not know how long they had been walking. All he knew was that the heat beating down on them was harsh and unforgiving, and his clothes were now soaked to their core. Surely the camp couldn't be that much farther.

He fought off a wave of dizziness as he struggled to maintain his pace. Aside from Ulrik and Vorax, the others' breathing was becoming louder, the air punctuated by groans of discomfort and repeated curse words out of Skyrar's mouth. This was a harsh endurance test like nothing Morvin had ever experienced, but he was determined not to fail.

It should have been the middle of the night by now, but the light around them told Morvin otherwise, something his body fought against.

"Would it not be a good idea to take some rest soon?" Morvin asked.

"I agree with the Dwarf," Skyrar said, stopping immediately.

Morvin smirked. Clearly she had not wanted to be the first person to suggest this.

"It will take us an age to get there if we keep stopping,"

Ulrik growled. There was an unforgiving darkness in his eyes, one that showed no signs of lifting.

"If we collapse, then we will need to stop for even longer," Skyrar spat back.

"We can stop and rest when we are farther along our tracks." Ulrik turned and kept walking.

"I think Skyrar is right," said Vorax. "I can carry on, but we don't want to be in a position where we are carrying each other."

Damour looked around anxiously. "I don't think it's best to stop here, though. We are frightfully open," he added, taking a handkerchief from his tunic and mopping his head with it. "It is not just the terrain we need to be mindful of."

"As much as I want to rest, if Darmour is saying it is not safe, then maybe we should carry on, just a little farther," Tarin said. "I know it is not what any of us want."

"The dangers that lie farther ahead of us are surely no different than those we face here, as long as we have our wits about us," Morvin said. They had been walking for many hours and were in dire need of a rest and some food.

"Even the Dwarf agrees with me," Skyrar pointed out, reminding Morvin just how endearing she was. "I am not walking another step until we take a short rest and replenish ourselves." She sat down on a small mound of sand where a flat rock poked from. "At this moment in time, I don't give two shits if you go on without me."

Morvin crouched, letting the bottom of the barrel touch the sand before ducking under the bars. The relief from the weight was incredible and he almost fell over as he was used to leaning forward to counteract the weight. "Looks like we are stopping then." Morvin rolled his neck and squeezed his shoulders through his sodden tunic, relieved that the strain on his back was lifted.

"I am telling you, I don't think this is a good idea, something doesn't feel right," Darmour protested, but Vorax was already placing the other barrel on the ground to join the others.

"What harm will a short break do us?" Zerina asked.

"Ask him that." Darmour nodded to a skull that sat embedded in the sand beside Zerina. It was human and devoid of any flesh.

"Likely someone who got lost in the desert," Zerina said. "I am not a damsel in distress, Darmour. You know this. I do not scare easily."

Ulrik turned and stared into Zerina's eyes, his disapproval clear for all to see. She remained unflinching as she stared back. Ulrik was one of the most aggressive people Morvin had ever had the displeasure of meeting, and other than showing how apt he was with a blade, there were no other endearing features to him. Morvin found it strange that someone as thoughtful and kind as Zerina would sail alongside him in the first place.

There was an intense moment between the two as Ulrik breathed heavily, his face shielded in the shadow from his tricorn hat. It wasn't enough to hide his scowl, however. Zerina was fierce in her own right, and showed no signs of intimidation.

"Fine," Ulrik growled. "We don't stay for long, though. Catch a quick rest and then we move forward. The sooner we reach Kesheria, the sooner we get out of this blasted sun."

Zerina nodded and sat where she stood, resting her hands behind her and tilting her head backwards. Ulrik simply stood and watched the group intently.

"Personality and looks," Skyrar sighed sarcastically under her breath.

"Captain, I still don't think it is a good idea to stay here. As I said, something just doesn't feel right," Darmour protested once more.

"Thank the rest of this group. I am not their captain, they have shown that," Ulrik snapped back.

Whilst the rest of the group sat to rest, Darmour chose to remain standing, watching out suspiciously around them.

"Will you sit down?" Skyrar spat. "Making me nervous. Look around us, there is nothing for miles. I am pretty sure if anything was around us, we would see it coming."

The ground around her shook and Skyrar's eyes shot wide open in confusion as the sand beneath her began to vibrate intensely.

"Skyrar, move back!" Darmour demanded.

Skyrar shot up quickly and away from her perch just as sand cascaded down the rock where she had been sitting.

The rock appeared to be growing in size.

Then, out of the sand, more black, rock-like matter emerged. It was long and thick, at the head of it a sharpened claw.

"Scorpion!" Darmour screamed. As the sand vibrated more, it poured down the sides as the large scorpion pushed itself up out of its shelter, fixing its big, black beaded eyes on the group. Its pincers were large enough to cut any of them in half.

Morvin had never seen anything like it. He shuffled backwards through the sand until he hit another rock that protruded out of the ground. To his horror, the ground also began to shake behind him.

"Fuck!" he cursed before clambering to his feet and

heading back towards the group. Out of the sand right where he had just been, a second giant scorpion emerged, snapping its claws in front of it. Pincer-like teeth pressed against one another as the scorpion shot its stinger towards Morvin.

The speed of it shocked Morvin as he darted to the side, trying his hardest to make sure he was not in range of another strike.

The first scorpion lunged towards Skyrar, and she was not quick enough. As the stinger jabbed her in the shoulder, she screamed out in pain before being lifted high into the air. Then she was slammed down into the sand right in between the scorpion's hooked claws. They snapped in anticipation as Skyrar pushed herself back to her feet, but she wavered on the spot as she struggled to fight the scorpion with the venom that now coursed through her.

A strange chattering of teeth was accompanied by a high-pitched noise as the scorpion's tail shot down at her once more. Morvin dived into the path of the scorpion, knocking Skyrar out of its trajectory. The strike barely missed Morvin. He counted himself lucky as he landed beside the injured shadow walker, who was bleeding heavily.

"You're going to be okay, lass," he told her. "Get her out of here!"

Vorax arrived first, waving her great axe in one hand to knock back the scorpion's tail. Zerina's arms glowed white-hot as though they were molten metal, and she launched a blast of fire magic at the scorpion. The magical energy bounced off the hardened shell, causing little damage. The flames, however, landed dangerously close to the barrels of powder.

"Careful!" Morvin screamed as he grabbed hold of

Skyrar and dragged her away. The barrels were too close to the fight. If they were to ignite in such close proximity, that would likely be the end for all of them.

"Hope you don't mind," Morvin said, taking one of Skyrar's daggers from her belt as the others squared off against the beasts. Skyrar was conscious but mumbling in a pained daze.

"Hold tight, lass." Morvin sprang to his feet and ran to help the others. To his left, Vorax, Zerina, and Darmour contended with the scorpion that had stung Skyrar. Ulrik and Tarin stood against the other. Ulrik had his cutlass raised above him, striking down whenever the scorpion lunged forward. Static energy caused Tarin's hair to stand on end as he summoned his storm magic between the palms of his hands. He pulled his hands behind him, then fired the blast forward. The magic connected with the claw of the scorpion before the bolt of energy jumped to the creature's opposite claw. The scorpion raised its body upwards as it recoiled back. It seemed that Tarin's magic had more of an effect on it than Zerina's fire magic had.

As it went crashing down, its stinger shot down towards Ulrik who brought down his cutlass against its hardened skin. His blade bounced off it as if he was striking stone, sparks flying in the air from the contact.

The sorption spun, crashing the side of its stinger into Ulrik. The pirate captain wrapped his arms around it, clinging on tightly. The scorpion swung its stinger around violently as it attempted to shake him off whilst at the same time striking down at Tarin. Tarin wearily dodged the strikes, unfurling another blast of storm magic into the creature's face.

"Its flesh is as hard as stone, what do we do?" Morvin asked as he sought to distract the scorpion.

"Aim for the eyes!" Darmour's voice boomed.

The scorpion's tail swung at Morvin again. He dodged to the side and jabbed Skyrar's dagger against it, but found it jammed against the hard surface, the pressure nearly snapping his wrist. Ulrik continued to be swung around wildly in the air as he held on to the stinger.

The scorpion lashed out with one of its claws, the outer edge of it smashing into Tarin and sending him rolling through the sand with an audible groan of pain. Th static energy around him failed as he was rendered unconscious in an instant.

Morvin ducked as the other claw came straight at him. With no other option, he charged forward at the face of the gargantuan scorpion, Ulrik's shadow darting around him. As the scorpion exhaled, Morvin could feel the wrath of its breath against his skin, its ginormous teeth clicking together frantically. The putrid smell knocked him sick, but Morvin pushed through this and jumped as high as he could, jamming the dagger into one of the shining black eyes of the scorpion.

The scorpion squealed as a strange white gunk escaped the eye and poured over Morvin's arm. It felt thick and sticky as Morvin brought his other hand up to grip the dagger, holding on tightly. The scorpion raised its body, its teeth snapping menacingly.

Ulrik let go of the stinger, rolling as he hit the sand before searching for his cutlass. When he saw it, he scooped it up from the ground and hurled it towards the now-exposed underbelly of the scorpion. With a loud crunching noise, the cutlass pierced the scorpion's skin. The beast wailed and waved its body from side to side as the sandy terrain was painted red. As the creature fell forward, Morvin dragged all his weight downwards on the dagger, again and again until he felt the blade tear through the scorpion's eye socket and down its face. The beast screeched once again before collapsing on its side, the chatter of its teeth slowing, its claws closing for one final time.

Morvin crumpled to the ground, pulling with him Skyrar's dagger. His beard stank from the innards of the scorpion's eye and he panted heavily from the fight. Ulrik offered him a gloved hand and pulled him to his feet, then yanked his embedded cutlass from the beast's belly.

The others continued to struggle with the second scorpion. Zerina fired blasts of molten flame at it over and over again, but it did not do anything to its rock-like skin, which appeared to be glowing red in places.

It launched a claw forward and Vorax brought her great axe down on it, sounding as though metal had struck metal. Her strength was enough to drive the claw and bury it into the sand where she held it in place for a moment. The scorpion was stronger, though, and as it flicked its claw from the sand, it tossed Vorax to the ground, causing her to drop her weapon.

"No!" Morvin cried.

Darmour went to help her under the cover of Zerina's magic, but the other claw snapped at him. He cried out in pain as the blade he was gripping dropped to the sand.

His hand was still attached to it.

Darmour dropped to the floor beside Vorax and clung to his arm as blood poured from him.

"Darmour!" Zerina cried. She stopped what she was doing and ran to aid him.

"Shit!" Ulrik cursed, sprinting as fast as he could.

Morvin trailed close behind, but he was not as quick. The world seemed to move in slow motion as the scorpion raised its stinger high once again. Darmour, Vorax, and Zerina huddled together on the ground. Ulrik sprinted towards them, roaring with anger, his cutlass raised high in the air.

"Stinger!" Morvin bellowed until his throat rasped and stung, sand lining the inside of his mouth.

As the scorpion brought its stinger down, Vorax leapt up at the last moment and grabbed it by either side, stopping it from connecting with any of them. It was as if the gods themselves granted her strength as she stared the creature dead in the eye and roared with rage, holding the stinger in place. Ahead of him, Morvin saw his wooden box, which lay open on its side. He knew that even though his new boom pistol was not finished, he had to try and use it.

He slid on his knees and scooped it up before reaching for the bottle of powder in his pocket. With a trembling hand, he tipped some of the powder in the end of the long shaft. This time it was reinforced with a studded metal band around the outside. He jammed one of the metal balls inside, then lifted the weapon tightly in both hands. All the while, Vorax strained to hold onto the scorpion's stinger, threatening to be pulled over at any moment. It looked like she was using every ounce of her strength to hold it in place.

"Keep her steady!" Morvin called, covering the sand as fast as he could. When he drew level with Vorax, he looked deep into the dark, beady eyes of the scorpion, then pulled the trigger.

With an almighty bang and a flash of light, the scorpion wailed and shrieked as Morvin closed his eyes, bracing himself to be hurled backwards. But this didn't happen. Instead, an ear-piercing shriek left the creature's mouth as the scorpion reared. Sections of its face blew high into the air, leaving nothing but a gaping hole where its eyes had been. Its cracked shell and chunks of flesh rained down on the group before the force of the blast forced the scorpion onto its back. Its legs continued to scurry in the air for a moment before its life ended in a pool of thick, treacle-like blood.

12

"Hold his arm still!" Zerina demanded as she pressed her hands down and channelled her magic to try and quell Darmour's pain.

Morvin was unable to tell if Zerina's magic was working, but he pressed down on Darmour's shoulders nonetheless. The pirate screamed in agony as a faint, pulsating glow flashed from Zerina's hands.

"Where's Tarin?" she asked.

"Unconscious," Morvin replied as he struggled against Darmour who was squirming around in pain. Tarin had planned this mission meticulously, and Darmour was the other tactician. He had the knowledge of Tarin's plan, too. It didn't bear thinking how it would affect the plan if they lost one of them, let alone both of them.

"Shit, I was hoping he might be able to help with the pain." Zerina grimaced as her magic flowed into Darmour's arm.

As Morvin watched over him, he noticed that Darmour's eyes had become sunken and purple, his face a ghastly pale grey that made him seem as though he was of the undead. "He's losing too much blood!"

"We need to stop the bleeding," Ulrik said, unbuckling his belt. He knelt on Darmour's arm who let out an almighty yelp and looped the leather belt around his forearm, pulling it tight. Darmour again screamed in pain.

"Zerina, can you reattach the hand with your magic?" Ulrik asked calmly.

"I'm not a fucking surgeon, Ulrik, you know more than any that my magic has limitations," Zerina shot back, her face showing a rare flash of frustration. "You're going to be okay, Darmour, I need you to be okay!"

Darmour's head lulled backwards as he drifted in and out of consciousness. He tried to speak but nothing other than a flurry of slurred words left his lips.

"We're going to lose him if we don't stop that bleeding," Morvin said. "Use your flame magic on his arm, Zerina, it will help." He had seen Dwarves lose digits and sections of hands whilst working in the forge.

"Of course, hold him tight." She focused on her hand which started to glow white-hot, causing Morvin to turn his head and shield his eyes.

"I am sorry, Darmour, but this is going to hurt, a lot." She pressed her hand against the bloody stump of his arm which now sat just above the wrist. Skin sizzled like fresh meat on a spit. If the sound of Darmour's skin sizzling and crackling under Zerina's flames wasn't nauseating enough, the smell was. Burning flesh curdled with a metallic taste in Morvin's mouth from his bust lip caused his stomach to heave. Darmour's eyes shot open, and he stared wide-eyed straight into Morvin's soul. What left his lips was the most ear-splitting roar of pain that Morvin had ever witnessed. Maybe it was because he was in close proximity, but

Darmour suddenly found a second wind of strength as he attempted to sit bolt upright. Morvin pressed down on him even harder, pushing him into the sand.

He feared that if he pushed any harder, he may cause Darmour further injury. "I am sorry, friend," he said, "this will be over soon."

Sand clung to Ulrik's sweat-covered face as he strained to keep Darmour's arm down, but Darmour pushed up against him as if he weighed nothing.

"Where's Vorax? I could do with a hand here," Ulrik said through gritted teeth.

Morvin looked around to find Vorax knelt beside Skyrar who appeared to be unconscious farther up from the group. "She's with Skyrar, we need to get to her, too."

Zerina pulled her hand away from Darmour's stump and for a few moments, his skin continued to bubble and sizzle. Darmour strained as he fought against the pain until he fell unconscious. Morvin released the pressure from his shoulders as Zerina rushed around and knelt beside his head, raising it slightly and resting it on her lap. She rubbed her hand down his cheek tenderly, her eyes welling with tears. Morvin wondered if the two were more than friends.

"You will be okay, Darmour. Rest now," she said as she began stroking her hand over his head.

"I'll go check on Tarin," Ulrik said.

Morvin got up quickly and rushed over to where Vorax was pressing some of Skyrar's torn clothing into her wound to stop the bleeding.

"If there's poison in there, we are going to have to try and get as much out as we can. The gods only know what that will be doing to her insides," Morvin said. "Roll her onto her side."

Vorax pulled Skyrar's body towards her own and

Morvin raised her blood-soaked cloak to see that there was blood seeping from her shoulder. Down her back, a translucent, pale-green liquid clung to her clothes, sand clinging to it like a potent cocktail.

"It's only a scratch," Skyrar said with slurred words.

Upon closer inspection, Morvin could see tracked veins stretching out from the wound. "The stinger went straight through, but I think there is some poison in there," he said. "We can get that bleeding under control, but we need to get that poison out of you." Morvin tore some of his sleeve off and pressed it into the wound at the back of her shoulder, directing Vorax to do the same at the front. Somehow, they had all survived the scorpion attack, but Morvin looked on nervously as he wondered just how many giant scorpions lay hidden in the sand. Surely they could not survive another attack.

"Is she okay?" Tarin's voice came from behind Morvin. He was bleary eyed and held a raised hand to his ribs, a streak of blood running from his bottom lip. He wore a worried expression as he saw the damage that Skyrar had sustained.

"I think there is venom in the wound," Morvin said. "Is there anything you can do?"

Tarin nodded. "I'll grab my effects. I have needle and thread to stitch up her shoulder and a syringe to extract what poison I can." He paused, turning to Morvin. "Darmour. Which hand did he lose?" he asked quietly so that only Morvin could hear him.

"His leading one," Morvin answered.

"Shit." Looking crestfallen, Tarin went to retrieve his medical instruments.

"You hear that, lass?" Morvin maintained the pressure with his left hand as he knelt behind Skyrar and brushed her hair back from her face. She was no paler than usual, with Morvin noticing some light freckles on her cheek. She looked at peace as if she were sleeping, not like she had been impaled with the stinger of a giant scorpion. "You are far too stubborn to let a little wound like this stop you," he told her.

When darkness finally greeted them, it gave them a brief reprieve from the harsh heat that the sun had brought down on them. Using the carcass of the scorpions, the group managed to fashion two stretchers, one for Skyrar and one for Darmour. Morvin and Vorax carried Skyrar, with Zerina and Ulrik insistent on carrying Darmour. There was no time to rest; Skyrar and Darmour's conditions were too dire. Not only did they need to carry them, they had two barrels of the powder to carry as well. One was strapped to Morvin's back, his Dwarven constitution meaning he was a natural choice to carry the powder. Vorax was the same with her sheer size making it logical that she carried the second barrel.

With Skyrar, Darmour, and the two barrels to carry, they moved far slower than any of the party would have liked, the soft sand providing a difficult terrain to navigate.

Tarin led the march through the darkness, holding a gas lamp aloft to light their way. Given how harsh the sun had been to them during the elongated day, Morvin was grateful for some coldness and was in no hurry to seek warmth.

"We shouldn't have too much farther to travel. I think if we can carry on through the night, we should reach the camp by the morning," Tarin announced.

"I hope their healers are able to help," Zerina said. "There is only so much my magic can do. Darmour is in need of a surgeon."

"This wasn't part of the plan, Tarin," Ulrik growled, his displeasure clear in his tone.

"Indeed, it was not," the mage replied, his focus steady on the darkened path in front of them. "We are a lot weaker than I would have liked us to be when we reached the camp. All we can do is re-evaluate when we arrive. For now, our focus needs to be getting help for Darmour and Skyrar."

For a time, the only sound was that of heaving, steady breaths as the party focused on navigating the darkness, the sand making their movement slower, especially given the additional weight they were carrying.

"That weapon of yours, I have never seen anything like it," Vorax said from behind Morvin, a welcome reprieve from the sound of their boots on the sand and stone.

"I am just glad it worked." Morvin looked down to his side where his boom pistol was strapped to him. To his relief, it had not broken apart like his first one. The riveted band that wrapped around the end, middle, and bottom of the cylindrical tube had reinforced the steel enough to be able to take the force of the metal bearing that was shot from it. Still, his shoulder smarted from the recoil, but he had sanded down the wood of the handle to make it as smooth as possible. He knew his shoulder would be bruised come daylight. He had left his boom pistol loaded and ready, just in case he needed to use it again.

"It really is quite the remarkable weapon you have created. How long has it taken you?" Tarin asked, casting his eyes over the strange device.

"It took me years to engineer it, to design it, and combine the three parts – the cylinder, the handle, and the flint, which acts as a trigger. I thought I was mad when I had the idea, but even when it was constructed, it took me that time again to develop the powder I needed to harness its power." Morvin sighed. "It took so long, but I was determined to make it work."

The wind was picking up now. Sand whipped up around them as they walked, further hindering their pace as they continued to trek with Darmour and Skyrar in tow.

"It is all I have focused on since my wife and son died in battle," Morvin continued. "It is what has kept me going all this time."

"True, your boom pistol is a remarkable piece of craftsmanship, but I can't express the importance of this powder that you have invented. It could change the world," Tarin said.

"True, but that is not why I wanted it. I needed the powder to power my weapon. So that I could use it to get my vengeance. The explosion that brought you to me was fated. I would not be here now, hoping that the rudest woman I have ever met makes it through the night."

"You have such a way with words," Skyrar croaked as she stirred from her unconsciousness.

"You're awake!" Morvin smiled. "Had us worried for a moment there."

The party stopped walking as Tarin moved to Skyrar's side to check on her, producing a flask of water to her lips which he helped her drink.

"I'm not a cripple," she spat as she grimaced, sitting herself up on the makeshift stretcher. Morvin and Vorax set her down, happy to take a break.

"If you insist." Tarin smiled. "You are lucky to be alive, we all are. If not for Morvin and his boom pistol, that scorpion would have got the better of us all."

"I bet there are not many who have taken the sting of a giant scorpion before and lived to tell the tale across these lands," Skyrar said with a grin before wincing once again. She pulled at her torn tunic to see that a bloodied bandage had been wrapped around her chest and shoulder.

"The stinger went straight through you," Morvin said. "If that had not happened, then it is likely you would not be with us now. Tarin cleaned your wound as best he could and stitched you up. Glad you are okay, lass."

Skyrar looked coy beneath the gentle glow of Tarin's lamp. "Thanks," she said. "Not only for patching me up, Tarin, but to you too, Morvin, for coming to my aid. It takes either bravery or stupidity to leap into the path of a giant scorpion."

Morvin leant forward, an air of seriousness on his face. "Was that" – he paused for dramatic effect – "a compliment?" His serious face grew into a wide smile. "Tarin, did you hear that? The lass just complimented me, an old Dwarf."

Tarin and Vorax laughed along with Morvin and the atmosphere lifted slightly.

"Well, don't let it get to that big head of yours. I am sure I will be back to my brooding self by the morning. I do have one request though."

"Go on," Morvin replied, intrigued at what Skyrar would ask of him.

"As powerful as that weapon of yours is, you cannot continue to call it a boom pistol, it sounds childish."

"I'm quite happy with it," Morvin said, placing his hand over his weapon as if shielding its ears from Skyrar's harsh words.

"Skyrar is right," Vorax said.

"I am afraid I would have to agree with these two," Tarin added.

"Not you, too." Morvin shook his head. "You weren't

complaining about what it was called when it was saving all of our lives!"

"A fine weapon like that deserves a name," Tarin continued. "Like one you would give to someone or something that you cherish more than anything in this world. Something that will not only motivate you to wield it but will strike fear into the pits of your enemies' bellies."

A spark ignited in Morvin's head and in an instant, Tarin's words resonated with him. What came with that was a name, one that would serve to motivate him but also strike fear into his enemies. Morvin only knew of one person who held a fury and strength on the battlefield that could rival his boom pistol, and he knew straight away what to call it.

"Herelda," he said. "I shall call her Herelda."

13

When they saw the black and gold colours of Askela hoisted at the top of flagpoles in the distance, they knew that they had finally made it to the camp. The night's walk had been a rugged test of endurance, but they had persevered, and they had made it. Skyrar had remained too weak to walk for most of the journey, and Darmour's uncertain condition had them all on edge.

Rows upon rows of tents sat in the sand, stretching farther than Morvin could have imagined, with posts where clusters of soldiers stood watch. Beyond the camp, a large stone wall protected Kesheria Keep at the top of a hill made of sand.

Morvin's chest thundered at the sight. This was closer to the king than he had ever been.

He was so close to revenge.

As planned, they were to present as a group of mercenaries upon their arrival. What they had not anticipated, however, was Darmour losing his hand and Skyrar having her shoulder impaled by a venomous stinger.

"Remember, we need to stick together as best as possible," Tarin said with a stern glare.

"That's easier said than done when we have wounded members in the party," Morvin replied.

When they reached a checkpoint, a group larger than their own greeted them. They all wore tunics of the king's colours, black with a yellow band across the middle between the stomach and the chest.

Tired and weary from their journey, the group staggered to the front, stopping when one of the soldiers raised her hand.

"Halt," the woman said, her hazel eyes looking untrustingly over the group. She was middle aged with white hair down to her shoulders, and judging by the stern look on her face, she was battle weary. A battle scar had permanently curled part of her lip downwards like a fish on a hook. "Where do you hail from and what business do you have here?" she said, a gruff growl in her voice. She was of a strong build with a polearm strapped to her back, the tip of which held a large spear.

Tarin forced himself to the front of the group, his legs near buckling as he stood in front of the woman. The other soldiers stood behind her with their hands planted on the hilts of their swords.

"We are here at the request of the general. He asked for reinforcements, requested for mercenaries to come and help in the war, anyone who can fight. Wanting to do my part for the war against the Zarubians, I have done what I could to recruit this fine group of fighters to pledge our swords to the King's War." Tarin reached inside his tunic, pulled out a ruffled parchment, and passed it to the woman.

She opened up the soggy, blood-soaked parchment to

see it stained with sweat and blood as well as being torn in places. It did, however, bear the conscription notice from General Precian as well as his signature and stamp.

The woman lowered the letter and cast her scowling eyes over the ragtag group. Zerina and Ulrik stood holding up a barely conscious Darmour, his blistered stump hanging over Ulrik's shoulder. To the side of them, Vorax stood proudly to attention, as if marching through a desert with a barrel full of powder in a full suit of Elven armour had barely affected her. Aside from her short hair being slicked back with sweat, she looked relatively unblemished. Next to her stood a weary looking Skyrar, her shoulder sagging on the left side. Her clothes were torn, and she had large purple bags under her eyes, but at least she was back on her feet.

The woman's eyes then dropped to the Dwarf who stood scowling at her. He was sweaty and bedraggled, his thick, plaited beard unkempt and frayed. Then her eyes came back to the tired old man, his sodden clothes sagging at the neck, his breathing heavy and his face burned from the sun.

"Fuck sake," she bellowed, rolling up the parchment. "They must be really scraping the barrel if you are here to help us. Look at the fucking state of you."

The group behind her burst into raucous laughter and Morvin felt his cheeks burn with a flash of anger. If there was one thing that he detested, it was being laughed at. He went to step forward but found Skyrar's hand firmly placed in front of him. He looked at her and noticed her cheeks reddened, too, but she simply shook her head at him before looking forward once again.

"This journey has been unforgiving and relentless," Tarin told her. "We unfortunately garnered the attention of two giant scorpions just last night. As you can see, my mercenaries are in need of rest and, if possible, these two could do with the attention of your healers. Once rested, I assure you that we will do what we can to fight the King's War." Tarin ended by bending one of his knees and bowing his head. "We will do what we must for Levanthria." Morvin couldn't help but smile. After all, Tarin was not lying with that last sentence.

"Giant scorpions?" the woman snarled. "The seven of you fought off two of them?" She almost snorted as she choked on her words.

Tarin nodded. "This is why we look this way, why two of my people are injured. You have our papers, you can see for yourself that we are here at the request of the general."

The white-haired soldier looked sternly over the group once more, shaking her head on more than one occasion. There was a tense silence for longer than Morvin would have liked, but he stood, shoulders back, fists clenched tightly.

"Very well," she said. "Vior, Travor, escort the injured to the healers. The rest of you come with me."

One of the men went to aid Darmour, while the other approached Skyrar.

"Fuck off, I can walk myself," Skyrar snapped.

"I need to go with Darmour," Zerina protested as one of the burly guards took Ulrik's place under Darmour's arm.

"Listen," the woman spat, less than impressed with Zerina's response. "If you want to keep that unblemished face of yours that way, I suggest you learn very quickly how to follow orders of a captain." Her teeth were clenched and for a moment, Morvin didn't know who was at risk, the captain or Zerina. Zerina's hair whipped up as if a breeze had taken hold of her, but she quickly regained composure.

Morvin knew that the worst thing she could do right now was expose herself as a sorceress.

"And from now on, you address me as Captain Xerij," the woman said sternly, her eyes darting from one member of the group to the next. "Do you understand?"

"Yes, Captain," Tarin answered promptly, turning his head to the rest of the group who remained silent. It was only when he gave them a look of displeasure and shook his head did the ragtag group mumble their agreement. Not in unison, but out of sync like a disjointed choir.

"Better," Captain Xerij sighed. "This way."

As Skyrar and Darmour were escorted in another direction, the rest of the group followed Captain Xerij through camp, passing a multitude of weary soldiers along the way, each of them with a fixed, untrusting stare on the group. Morvin felt eyes burn into him deeply but chose to ignore it, keeping his head raised high, his beard nearly trailing along the ground.

"A fucking Dwarf and an Elf, what next?" a deep voice heckled as a soldier spat in front of them. The hostility towards them was uncalled for, Morvin felt. It was not like the soldiers *knew* that they were here with the sole intention of killing the king.

Morvin had the strong urge to step to the side and slam his fist into the man's face, but was disrupted when Captain Xerij suddenly stopped at a crossroads within the war camp.

"Your wounded will be treated on the southern front of camp," she said, pointing down the sand-kissed track. "Only then will we assess whether either of them are fit for active service."

"Captain," Tarin interrupted, "would it be wise to send

away two good fighters when the king has asked for reinforcements?"

"If they can't fight, it's just more mouths to feed. They
will be free to leave in that case. But given the state you
arrived here in, I doubt they would survive on their own."
She beckoned them to keep moving. "This way. I want your
weapons and effects inspected before you join the ranks."

She led them through the maze of the war camp, where
tents were lined up in orderly rows, branching out from the
path that ran all the way around the camp. Soldiers were
either training or heading into their tents to rest. Every
soldier they saw looked gaunt, tired, and generally run-
down. There wasn't any sound of idle conversation, just the
occasional bellow from a captain calling their soldiers to
formation, followed by the crescendo of the soldiers
replying in unison. They looked exhausted as they trained,
but they did seem well organised and prepared. A faint,
sickening musk hung in the air, clinging to the camp like an
unwanted gift. It was the type of stench one would expect
to find with so many people living in such close proximity.

They continued to pass through the camp until they
reached a tent that was larger than the rest. It was cream in
colour, or at least it used to be. Mould crept up the sides,
like blackened veins under corrupted skin. Pulling back the
cloth at its entrance, Captain Xerij motioned for the group
to follow her inside. "Leave your belongings there" – she
pointed at a dirty table – "and line up in front of me."

Tarin and Vorax led by placing the two barrels of
powder down first. Tarin let out a large gasp of relief from
no longer bearing the weight. The rest of the group placed
their weapons in front of the barrels. Morvin pulled the
strap that Herelda was attached to and raised it over his
shoulder.

"What is that?" the captain asked. She tried to pick up Herelda but struggled with the sheer weight of it.

"That is my weapon. Works like a crossbow, nothing more," Morvin answered. He didn't know how much information was too much, but figured telling the truth – more or less – would be best for now.

The captain examined the peculiar contraption with a quizzical stare. "It doesn't look like a crossbow."

Morvin shrugged. "It's a Dwarven thing."

She looked over Herelda one final time before placing it back on the table. "Very well," she said. "And the barrels?"

"Both contain supplies for our journey." Tarin spoke a little too quickly for Morvin's liking.

"Open them," she demanded.

Tarin did as asked, using one of the swords to pry the lid off.

Captain Xerij's eyes widened and Morvin felt an air of nervousness come over him. If they were rumbled, how would they explain the powder they had brought into camp?

"Interesting," Captain Xerij said as she reached into the barrel. From it, she retrieved a bottle of whisky. Underneath bottles of liquor, the powder had been glamoured to look like rice.

"Thought it would help raise the spirits of the soldiers, maybe even pull them on our side," Tarin explained.

Morvin chuckled to himself with Tarin's play on words. The mage was so calm and collected as he spoke, like he had rehearsed this scenario in his head ten times over.

The captain bit down on the cork and pulled it out of the bottle, smelled the contents, then took a swig of the whisky. She hissed and laughed before standing up straight and offering a wry smile.

"I think they will approve," she said. "You can distribute them once you are dressed."

Morvin sucked in air between his teeth and breathed out a suppressed sigh of relief. The captain took another swig of the whisky before placing the bottle back inside the barrel.

"You may be mercenaries, but you still need to be in uniform like everyone else," the captain said, resuming her commanding tone. "Strip," she ordered.

The others set about removing their clothing as directed, but Morvin stood there, looking around nervously.

"In front of everyone?" he asked.

The captain sighed. "We've all seen them before, don't worry."

Morvin removed his tunic and stood in line with the rest of the group whilst Captain Xerij inspected tunics that were in a pile on a table at the far side of the tent. One by one, she called the members of the group over and handed them a bundle of clothes which included pants, tunic, and a chainmail bodice.

"You wear your mail at all times," she told them. "And no one" – she paused, eyeing the group up as they dressed – "and I mean no one gets close to King Athos. Do you understand?"

"I already have armour," Vorax said, pulling the large tunic over her. "It is stronger than this chainmail. I will wear your tunic, but not the chainmail."

Captain Xerij stood in front of the towering Elf and looked up at her unflinchingly. "Very well," she said.

Morvin tucked his legs into his new trousers before pulling the chainmail bodice over himself. It was cold against his skin, with the mail plucking some of his chest hair. Once it was on, he threw his tunic over the top, biting down on the resentment that choked his throat at wearing the king's colours.

"When will we be able to check on our friends?" Zerina asked as she looked over the chainmail with a puzzled expression. Vorax helped her by turning it the right way around and placing it over her head.

"When the healers are done. You can use this tent to rest for tonight. When you get your postings tomorrow, you will be assigned your quarters and duties."

"If I may, we were told our group would be kept together," Tarin said, stepping towards the captain.

Her face erupted with anger, and in flash, she had knocked Tarin on his arse. "Listen, old man, I don't give two shits what you were told. You turn up here in the state that you did, you are lucky I have given you tunics and mail at all."

"There's no need for that captain," Morvin growled. "He was only – "

The captain's face turned from red to a purplish blue, so bright that Morvin feared her head may explode. "Speak out of turn again, Dwarf, and I will have your tongue," she spat.

He glared at her as he helped Tarin back to his feet.

"I'd learn pretty quick how things work in an army," she told them. "If someone with rank gives you an order, you listen. You are not mercenaries anymore, you are the king's forces." With that, she turned and left, near ripping the cloth door from the rest of the tent.

"What a lovely lady," Morvin huffed. "You okay?" He patted Tarin on the back as the mage straightened himself up.

"I like her," Ulrik said. Morvin had to do double-take, as he had never seen Ulrik without his tricorn hat on. His long dark hair was wavy and unkempt, falling beyond his shoulders.

"We need to find out if the others are okay," Zerina said.

Tarin shook his head sadly. "For now, we need to stay here, keep our heads down, and not antagonise Captain Xerij."

"I think you two have already failed at the latter," Vorax said with smile.

"It's okay for you," Morvin laughed. "You are twice the size of everyone else." "Makes her a bigger target," Ulrik said.

Zerina wore a concerned expression, and Tarin placed a comforting hand on her shoulder. "In the morning, we will ask after Skyrar and Darmour," he told her gently. Then he piled up his dirty clothes and placed them by one of the barrels where he lay down, resting his head. "We need to bide our time and win favour. That is the only way we are going to get into that keep and close enough to the king."

14

Morning was announced by the short, sharp blast of a horn. Morvin stirred as if being woken by the calm that dawn brought, with the rest of the group jolting upright and reaching for weapons as if they were under attack.

He had slept lightly by his standards, but strangely found the surface of the sand comfortable. Even if his hair and beard were now filled with the tiny orange grains, giving his beard a nice ginger tinge to it.

"Best not keep the captain waiting," Tarin said. He wasted no time in heading to the front of the tent and pulling back the doorway.

Bright sunlight lit up the darkened tent, causing the group to shield their eyes and curse him.

"Fuck, not everyone wakes as spritely as you, mage," Ulrik said with a scowl, looking as though he was ready to strike him.

"Do not address me as mage," Tarin fired back assertively, "not unless you want our cover blown. Spellcasters are kept away from everyone else in these camps. We need to be as close together as possible."

Ulrik clenched his jaw tightly, the leather of his gloves tightening as he clenched his fists.

"My contact assures me that our postings will be part of the guard duty. That should help us, as we will be in the same barracks, and we will be working in shifts. That will allow us time to map the camp out. During that time, my contact will work on us being drafted to guard the keep which will get us closer to the king."

"Come, Ulrik, let's find our postings and see how Darmour is," Zerina said, exiting the tent first. Ulrik sighed and followed her, with Vorax, Morvin, and Tarin close behind. They came to an abrupt stop outside the tent when they found Captain Xerij waiting for them on the pathway. Skyrar stood beside her, wearing the black and gold tunic, but no chainmail.

"Skyrar!" Tarin beamed before collecting himself. "Captain," he added, "we were just on our way to find you for our postings."

"I have them here." Captain Xerij unfurled some parchment in her hand. She wore a tired expression, and Morvin wondered if she had been up through the night.

"You two" – she pointed at Vorax and Ulrik – "you're on patrol."

Vorax and Ulrik nodded their heads in silence.

"You will join the healers," Captain Xerij continued, pointing at Tarin. "Skyrar tells me you stitched her shoulder up. I've seen it. Impressive work. You will be put to use there."

"Captain –" Tarin began.

"Speaking of which, Skyrar has been posted to our scouts. The healers have deemed her worthy of service."

Skyrar shook her head and rolled her eyes. Luckily her display of petulance was out of Captain Xerij's line of sight.

Next, the captain looked at Zerina. "You are to help with distributing rations," she said. "And you . . ." She lowered her eyes to Morvin. "You are on shit shovelling duty."

"Perhaps my friend here would be better served working in the armoury," Tarin objected.

The captain's nostrils flared. "He will go where I tell him. Won't you, Dwarf?"

Morvin remained silent, biting down on his pride. He knew what she was doing, but he was not sure if it was him personally she had taken a disliking to for answering her back the night before, or if it was because he was a Dwarf. He wanted to protest, but he did not want to give her the satisfaction.

"Aye, Captain," was all he said.

Captain Xerij, looking disappointed at not getting the reaction she wanted from Morvin, rolled up her parchment and placed it in the belt of her tunic. "Follow me. I will show you where you will be based."

"Remember, keep your heads down and wait for the opportunity. No matter how long it takes," Tarin muttered under his breath. "Our postings are not ideal, but once I have met with my contact, I am sure I can get us moved."

"Easy for you to say," Morvin growled under his breath. "You're not going to be shovelling shit."

"How is Darmour?" Zerina asked the captain as they made their way through camp.

"The healers are still working on him. Hopefully they will be finished with him in another day or so. Then we will see what he is capable of."

One by one, Captain Xerij dropped each of the group at various points around the camp. They were spread out further than Morvin would have liked, and judging from Tarin's expression, the mage was displeased as well.

They followed the captain like obedient dogs feigning wagging their tails as if they were grateful for their postings. Soon, only Morvin remained, keeping pace with Captain Xerij as best he could. As he walked, he stared at the back of the captain's head, imagining hurling a rock at her skull.

When they reached the outer edge of the camp, it was to find a group of men relieving themselves into the sand.

"Captain," one of them said in greeting. He had short blond hair and bright-blue eyes, and was of an athletic build. Morvin could tell simply by the way he carried himself that he held a higher rank of some sort. His shoulders were broad and he stood straight with his chin slightly raised, an air of arrogance around him. He wiped his hand on the next soldier's sleeve when he was finished, and to Morvin's surprise, the second man didn't react.

"Captain," Captain Xerij replied.

"And what do we have here?" the blond man sneered patronisingly. "I didn't know they allowed children in camp." He leant forwards, feigning getting a better look at Morvin. "Ugly bastard for a child, no wonder his mother sent him away." He laughed, and the other soldiers followed suite.

Morvin felt a flash of anger burn in his belly and found his jawline tightening.

Keep your head down, he thought to himself. He could not react, no matter how strong the temptation.

Captain Xerij puffed out her chest. "I am showing our latest reinforcements where he will be working," she said in a stern voice, her eyes unmoving. She did not seem happy to be in the presence of this man.

"Now, now, Xerij, no need to be so hostile with me. Let the past stay in the past," he said pompously.

"It is in the past, Reve. Doesn't mean I have to like you," she fired back. "Now, if you are done here, fuck off."

"No need to be like that," Captain Reve said playfully. "We may be equal in rank, but you should know your place just like the rest of these dogs." He lowered his eyes to Morvin. "And children." He stepped past Xerij and waved a hand dismissively as he walked off with the rest of the group.

"What a prick," Morvin said.

"He certainly is," Captain Xerij replied, staring into the back of Reve's head in the same way Morvin had been staring at her on their long walk here. She snapped herself out of it, and Morvin couldn't help but wonder what she was thinking.

"Right, this is your posting. It's quite simple. The shit is over there. There is your cart and shovel. You will clear up the shit and move it away from camp. This place is bad enough without the putrid smell of bowels."

Morvin closed his eyes for a moment, wishing he was anywhere else in the world right now.

"You do your job, you get rations at the end of the day."

"And if I don't?"

"Then you will be treated like a coward and cast out in the desert in disgrace."

As tempting as that was, it would not get Morvin any closer to the king, and he knew that he was going to have to dig deeper than ever before to keep his head down and get on with the horrendous task that had been placed upon him.

"Is there a problem?" she asked.

"No, Captain."

"Good. I'd suggest you get to it. There is a lot of shit to get through. You will be able to see the path where the others wheel their carts." Without so much as a goodbye, Captain Xerij left Morvin and made her way back into camp.

Deflated, Morvin sighed. Why could he not have been put on patrol with the others? Why could he not have been placed in the armoury as Tarin had suggested? He felt appreciative for Tarin stepping in for him, even if his request had fallen on deaf ears.

The smell was more and more putrid the closer Morvin stepped towards it. Piles of faeces dotted around inside a makeshift fence that seemed to serve as a poorly made latrine. Reluctantly, Morvin took the small cart and wheeled it towards the excrements of the soldiers. He stared for a moment, psyching himself up.

"It's not going to shovel itself," a cracked voice said, breaking Morvin's stare.

Morvin turned to see an older man with long white hair, his scalp visible through the whisps. He was thin, his skin sagging against his cheekbones. He wore the same tunic as everyone else, although his hung off him as if he wore the tunic of someone far larger.

"The smell is the worst part, but you soon get used to it." He smiled, then Morvin noticed he also had the handles of a cart in his hands. "I have not seen you before, and judging by your horrified face, I am guessing that you are new to this camp."

"What makes you think that?" Morvin said dryly.

"Tend to send the ones who are not traditionally suited for battle." He paused, eyeing up Morvin's thick, strong frame. "That, or you pissed off the wrong captain."

"She seems to have a general dislike to my kind,"

Morvin said, inspecting the shovel as he tossed it into the cart. The metal was stained, cracked, and rusted.

The old man nodded. "The captains are the highest rank we have this side of the camp. They're summoned every few days to report back to the higher-ups. It's the captains that call the shots around here. I learned to keep my mouth shut and do as I am told. Besides, if we don't clear up this shit, who will? Think about how bad the camp would become if we stopped working." He shuddered at the thought. "I tell myself this is one of the most important jobs with maintaining the camp." The scrawny man smiled through dirty, stained teeth.

"There's a dozen other jobs I would prefer over this," Morvin growled. He was not quite sure what he expected when they infiltrated the camp, but this was not it.

"Anyways, it was nice to meet you." The man's teeth whistled as he spoke. "You're more than welcome to work alongside me. I can show you the ropes. Not that there is much to learn. Shovel some shit here, shovel some shit there, and move the shit somewhere else." The man pushed his cart to one of the piles of excrement, whistling a tune to himself as he took up position and started filling his cart. "Name's Cork, if you are interested, that is."

"Morvin."

"Come fill your cart and I will show you where we are dumping it." Cork pointed out to the barren sands beyond the camp. "It's best part of a mile that way. The farther away, the better."

"Is it not dangerous out there?" Morvin asked, his memory of the scorpions all too clear.

"Nah, there are always soldiers on patrol. I've been here for nearly seven years. Four of them I've been in this camp, doing this."

Morvin reluctantly got to work filling his cart, fighting back the bile that stung the back of his throat every time he took a breath. Not only was the smell rancid, but the sound of the excrement landing in the cart alone was enough to cause Morvin to gag. When the two of them had filled their carts, Morvin followed behind Cork as he headed up a path formed in the sand. This side of the desert, the sand in the path was more mud-like in consistency, as if something had been done to treat it. It certainly made the task of pushing the cart easier, even if it was still difficult.

Cork appeared to be in a particularly good mood as he whistled his tune, even giving little jig with his hips every once in a while. Morvin merely focused on stopping himself from vomiting, opting to breathe shallowly through his partially opened mouth rather than his nose. It was the only way he found that he could survive the acrid, repugnant smell.

After what felt like an eternity, the pair reached the end of the path. It was clear where they were to empty the carts, as a large hole had been dug into the sand. It was filled with excrement and accompanied by the dull roar of flies buzzing around and feasting on the stewed spoils.

Morvin pushed his cart to the edge of the pit and tipped the contents out, which sloshed and splashed as it landed, causing his stomach to twist a little inside.

"Come on, it will be easier walking back now that we have offloaded," Cork said before whistling his tune and heading back down the path.

Morvin turned with his cart to follow. It was easier to see the keep from this side of camp, with it sitting atop a large bank of sand. The tents on this side were fewer, but Morvin could see the forms of soldiers walking along the wall on their patrols.

If only the others could get patrol duty in the keep.

Cork turned his head to check on Morvin and caught him staring at the fort.

"If you're lucky, you might end up cleaning the shit in there one day."

And just like that, a spark ignited inside Morvin. He needed to find a way to get that post. After all, even kings needed to take a shit from time to time.

15

For days Morvin focused on his post and doing exactly what was asked of him, ensuring that he made no mistakes. He filled his cart, he walked the path, he emptied his cart, and he returned. He had not seen much of the others given that he didn't spend long periods of time in camp. He was able to get in a few words here and there if one of them happened to be catching a toilet break to relieve themselves as he was filling his cart. He still had not heard of Darmour's condition and wondered whether or not he was recovering well from losing his hand. More than anything, Morvin just wanted to know if he was okay.

He had anticipated being able to meet with the others in the evenings for meals, but given the repulsive smell that clung to his tunic, he was forced to eat and sleep on the outer edges of the camp, away from everyone else.

Morvin had even seen Vorax and Ulrik on separate patrols as he travelled down the path to the shit pit, but was unable to exchange anything but a quick glance and nod. Ulrik barely even acknowledged him.

Still, Morvin had done exactly what he intended to do:

work hard and not complain. No matter how difficult, no matter how tired he felt, he gritted his teeth and got on with his job, because he knew he was working towards something greater.

His cheeks bore a flash of red where he had caught the sun. His eyes felt heavy and his legs were aching with fatigue. Morvin was on his fourth run of the day as he set about shovelling the excrement into his cart. He knew that another one or two runs and he would be able to rest and settle down for his evening rations. Cork had been right: in the short time he had being doing the job, the smell had become less offensive and more tolerable. At least, his stomach lurched and plunged far less now than when he had first started.

He was about halfway to filling up his cart when he heard the oncoming steps of soldiers. He carried on shovelling, only stopping when a familiar voice garnered his attention.

"Psst, Morvin."

Morvin stopped what he was doing to see Tarin entering the communal toilet. On this rare occasion, there was no one else around them.

"Tarin, any word from the others?" Morvin asked. "How's Darmour?"

"He is still not back with us, but should be any day now. The others seem to be settling in well to the posts. As far as I am aware, they have not caused any trouble. Even Skyrar seems content scouting ahead."

"Glad you are all enjoying yourselves," Morvin replied, feeling somewhat downcast at the thought.

Tarin looked down at Morvin whose tunic was beyond filthy. "I am so sorry you ended up with this post."

"Someone's got to do it," he said sarcastically, Cork's

words echoing in the back of his mind. "Have you heard from your contact yet?"

Tarin looked pensive and shook his head. "I am afraid not."

"Good job that I've got a plan then, eh?"

"Go on."

"Cork said that us shit tippers can be posted in the keep. He even said he has had to collect from the keep more than a few times." Morvin spoke in a hushed, excited voice. "I am going to bide my time, keep my head down, and one of these days, I will get my opportunity. All I need to do now is figure out how to get my powder inside."

"Interesting," Tarin mused. "That would be a good window of opportunity. Leave it with me, I will work on a plan on how to get the powder inside the keep."

"What's going on here?"

The pompous voice caused Morvin to curse under his breath.

Tarin and Morvin turned to see Captain Reve stood nonchalantly as he entered the toilet.

"Nothing sir, just catching up with a friend," Morvin answered.

"I wasn't talking to you, Dwarf," Captain Reve sneered.

"It is as he said, Captain. I have not seen my friend here since we were all posted," Tarin said politely.

"If I was you, I would be careful talking to such fish. It's one thing that he spends his days here cleaning up all our shit. It's another that he is a Dwarf." Reve spoke as if Morvin was not in proximity.

Morvin's nose flared, and he found himself puffing out his chest. What was it with these captains and the way they looked down on his kind? It was infuriating. Morvin chewed on his words for a moment before reaching for the handles of his cart. "I'll be getting back to work," he said though gritted teeth.

"Hold on," Reve demanded, walking towards Morvin.

Morvin was lucky his face was burnt from the sun, as it masked the flash of anger in his cheeks. He remained unmoved, his muscles tensing as Reve stopped in front of him.

Reve unbuckled his pants and took out his member before urinating on the sand just in front of Morvin's dust-covered boots. Sighing as he relieved himself, Reve wore an antagonising grin.

Morvin did not move. His teeth risked shattering as his jaw clenched in anger. His knuckles cracked and he stared defiantly at Reve, not wishing to show him any weakness even as Reve's urine splashed over his boots and up the bottom of his trousers.

Tarin, who stood just behind Reve, shook his head but remained silent, an ashamed expression on his face.

The most frustrating thing for Morvin was the knowledge that even with his size, he felt confident that he could beat Captain Reve to an inch of his life if he was given the opportunity. But because of his rank, because of his entitlement, the captain could walk around like this, doing what he wanted without a care in the world for any form of repercussions. The fact that King Athos Almerion allowed this to happen in his camp only fuelled Morvin's hatred towards him. The sooner he could get inside that keep, the better.

When Reve was done, he shook himself off, re-dressed himself, and gave Morvin a wry smile. "See, this Dwarf knows his place already. You need not waste your breath talking to him." He leant down and wiped his damp fingers on Morvin's tunic.

Morvin just accepted it. It was difficult, but he swallowed his pride and let Reve do what he wanted. He did not rise to the bait, despite the temptation to stove his head in there and then. To do so would be instant suicide, and knowing it would likely lead to his execution, Morvin simply turned back to the pile of faeces and finished filling up the cart.

Reve laughed to himself as he left, leaving Tarin and Morvin alone once more. Morvin was too angry to speak. He remained stony-faced and silent as he continued to work, choosing to take out his frustration with his shovel as he forcefully filled the cart.

"I am so sorry you had to endure that," Tarin said with an apologetic tone. "I will see what I can do about the powder. I will find a way to get it inside the keep. You do what you must to get access. It isn't the best situation, but it is all we have for now. Know that the intention and understanding was that we would all be kept together. I just need to find a way to get hold of my contact. This wasn't part of the plan." Tarin's shoulders slumped as he spoke, his face saddened. This was not the confident and joyful spellcaster that Morvin had become accustomed to, and that worried him.

Morvin, however, didn't make eye contact with Tarin. He focused on his job; it was the only way he could cope with the degradation. He felt too ashamed to utter another word. Tarin, respecting Morvin's need to be alone in this moment, left to head back to the healers' tent.

Morvin's thoughts stewed. He would remember this moment, he would remember the hostility that a captain of the king's army had shown towards him, and he would use how he was feeling to motivate him even further. He would not let his spirit be broken, he would not rise to the bait, he would simply continue his job as had been requested of him. No matter what.

The second the opportunity arose for him to clean the keep, he would take it with every ounce of him and show the world his unknown fury.

16

It was the end of another arduous day. Morvin was growing tired from going through the same awful routine every day.

Aside from the occasional nod as he passed patrols, Morvin kept himself to himself. It was how he wanted it to be. He avoided the others if they happened to be in the toilet area when he was. He didn't want to hear them apologising for his situation; however well-intended they were, it only made him more frustrated, which in turn made it even harder for him to keep a lid on his emotions.

Having just finished up with his last run of the day, Morvin placed his cart and shovel to one side where it would remain until the next day. It had been a few days since he'd had any contact with the others, and he could feel his frustration growing. The others seemingly had easier duties in camp than he did. His plan was to seek out Tarin, should the opportunity arise. He needed to know that their plan was moving forward.

"You have been awfully silent these last few days," Cork

said as he pulled up his own cart and left it to rest. Morvin had not seen Cork all day.

"Where have you been?" Morvin asked, his throat dry.

"In the keep! Got asked to carry out my duties in there today."

Morvin could be forgiven for feeling jealous. All this could end so quickly if he could just be given access.

"I don't mean to be rude, Morvin, but you smell foul. Even by my standards. When did you last clean yourself?"

"I haven't," he answered stonily. "Hasn't been our time to use the baths."

"You need to look after yourself," Cork scolded. "I know that we can only access the baths once a week, but maybe you should take my place today."

"Thank you," Morvin grumbled. Of course it made sense that the vile stench of the toilets would cling to his clothes, to his hair, even his beard, but Morvin had simply become too used to it to notice.

"The baths are just beyond the healers' tents. That's where they keep the clean water to tend to any soldier's wounds," Cork explained kindly. "I can show you where to go if you want."

"It's okay, I am sure I can find my way." Morvin trudged towards the healers' camp via the outer edge of the camp, not wanting to catch the attention of other soldiers who insisted on looking down on him as if he were inferior to them. All the same, he kept a steady eye out for Tarin or the others. He'd had nothing but shit and Cork to keep him company these last few days, and he felt as though he was slowly losing his sanity.

It didn't take long to find the medium-sized tent that appeared to be the bathing area. A group of soldiers were exiting it, their hair slicked back and wet, but they still appeared bedraggled with a variety of stubbled and bearded faces.

Morvin made his way towards the tent, hoping that no one else would be there. Inside, basins lined the canvas walls full of varying colours of water, depending on how much it had been used.

Morvin supposed it was better than nothing.

Although his tunic was in a disgusting state, at the very least he could give his muck-covered hands, face, and beard a wash.

Morvin removed his shirt and enjoyed the wash. The water wasn't cold, and it wasn't the freshest, but soon his skin was more visible save for the dirt that stained his fingernails, which remained even after scrubbing as best he could. He gave his beard a squeeze to release some of the excess water and felt fresh air touch his cleaner skin for the first time in a while. He savoured the moment, savoured the brief reprieve and freshness that the wash gave him, and appreciated in this moment that no one else was around. The temperature was still hot outside, and Morvin chose to toss his tunic and chainmail over his shoulder for the walk back to his quarters.

As he exited the tent, he saw Captains Xerij and Reve marching into the large healers' tent nearby. Knowing that Darmour was inside, he felt obliged to walk over and have a nosy.

Morvin peered around the edge of the pulled-pack tent flap. Darmour was standing at the foot of a bed, wearing the mail and tunic of Levanthria like everyone else. He had his good arm raised in a salute to the two captains. Aside from still being a shade paler than usual, he looked as if he was near enough back to full health following the loss of his hand.

"Captains," Darmour said, "I'd like to report that I am fit for duties and ready to be posted."

"We will be the judge of that," Captain Reve sneered. "We can't afford to have anyone in camp who can neither contribute nor fight."

Undeterred, Darmour answered, "I can assure you that I can do both."

"Was it your prominent hand that you lost?" Xerij asked. She was assertive in her approach rather than rude like Reve.

"Aye, Captain, it was. I can still fight with my right hand, though."

"I'm sorry, Captains, but this man is still not ready," a young female healer protested. "He is yet to be back to full health." She was delicately spoken and she wore white and gold robes, her sleeves rolled up to her elbows.

"Tell me, soldier, what is your name?" Reve asked, ignoring the woman.

"Darmour, Captain," he replied, bringing his arm down from his salute. Darmour was certainly better versed in addressing rank, something he had likely learned sailing under the command of a captain at sea. Morvin wondered if he had military experience prior to this as he continued to watch on.

"Very well, Darmour, follow me. I find it hard to see how a soldier with one eye and one hand could fight. I want to see what you are capable of." Reve turned and exited the tent.

Morvin stepped back and tucked himself behind the flap, not wanting to draw any attention to himself, especially from Captain Reve.

Darmour and Xerij followed, and they walked through the tents to a larger opening where soldiers congregated when they were not on duty. Morvin trailed behind them from a distance, a silent observer. He hoped he would have an opportunity to speak with Darmour.

"Gather round, gather round!" Reve demanded, waving his hands in the air before clapping to get the attention of the soldiers that were holding conversations with one another.

Morvin could tell by many of the soldiers' eyerolls and heavy sighs that they did not necessarily respect Captain Reve, although they always took care to do these things out of Reve's sight.

A large circle began to form around the captain, with Xerij and Darmour remaining on the outer edges. On the other end of the clearing, Morvin could see Vorax and Skyrar stood side by side, with Ulrik nearby. He had his arms folded and an unimpressed scowl on his face, but this was an expression that Morvin was used to with the pirate captain.

"I need some of you to step forward to duel Darmour here. I am even happy to take a few bets of rations. You see, we need to see if this man" – Captain Reve eyed up Darmour, clearly aware that the hungry soldiers would take part for the chance of some extra rations of food – "is able to fight. After all, would you want someone incapable of wielding a sword next to you in battle? I believe the man is more of a liability than a help, and as such, needs to crawl back to the hole that he came from. It would appear, however, that Captain Xerij does not agree. I would like to find out who is right." He grinned from beneath his eyes, an almost maniacal laugh leaving him. "And if we have a bit of entertainment, I am sure it will lift spirits."

The soldiers cheered and words were muttered over who they thought would come out of the duel. From what

Morvin could make out through the rising noise of the crowd, not many favoured Darmour. To be fair, Morvin could understand that based on his appearance. Darmour was an older man, having the appearance of someone in his late forties with his bald head and greying beard. He had a strong frame but had clearly lost weight whilst being under the care of the healers. Even though he had one eye covered with a patch and his right arm bandaged over the stump where his hand once was, Morvin still backed his friend.

Out of the crowd, a man stepped forward to challenge Darmour. He was of a slight build, but when he removed his tunic and chainmail, it was to reveal a torso rippled with muscles. He looked a good few years younger than Darmour.

"Here we go!" Reve beamed.

Darmour stepped forward without hesitation and removed his own tunic and mail. His body was less muscular and covered with thick, black hair. He clicked his neck whilst the other soldier raised his hand to force a cheer from the crowd.

"When you are both ready," Reve said in a calm, calculated manner.

The two men started circling one another, their fists clenched and raised as they weighed up who was going to make the first move. When Darmour's back faced Morvin, he saw that the pirate's back was covered in thick purple scars, some in large lines, some dotted in sporadic places. This man had seen many a fight.

The soldier jabbed a testing punch at Darmour who slapped this down with his one good hand. He stepped forward to lunge with his free arm but stopped himself when he seemed to remember he had no fist to strike with. The move left him open, and the soldier quickly knocked his arm away before throwing a punch into Darmour's midriff. Darmour let out a grunt but he took the blow, quickly turning and bringing his elbow down onto the soldier's arm.

The soldier pulled it back just in time before it bore the full weight of Darmour's blow, a strike that would have likely broken his arm. Before the soldier had time to react, Darmour stepped into the young man's space and threw a solid punch to his rugged jaw, followed by an elbow from his weaker arm, then another punch and another elbow. The soldier's head bobbed from side to side as Darmour connected multiple blows before a final one that sent the soldier falling backwards into the crowd.

The crowd fell silent as Darmour turned to face Captain Reve. "Does that answer any questions you have about my ability to fight?" he asked. He had barely broken a sweat.

Morvin couldn't help but smile. Darmour was quite clearly an experienced brawler, and thinking on Reve's challenge, he knew exactly who he would want by his side on the battlefield.

Reve's smile faltered as the soldiers started changing the tacks of the betting. "You and you, step forward," he demanded, pointing out two more men from the crowd. "Let's see how you do with two against one."

The two soldiers stepped forward without hesitation, one of them speeding at Darmour from behind and quickly raining down multiple blows to his head.

"Stop! This is an unfair fight!" Zerina's voice called out from the crowd as Morvin pushed his way through to get a better look. He couldn't see her but he recognised her soft tone. Then he noticed that Tarin had joined Skyrar, Vorax, and Ulrik in the crowd. Each of them watched intently, each looking as though they were fighting the urge to get involved.

Darmour managed to throw an elbow back, knocking one of the soldiers from on top of him just as the other ran forward and connected a boot to Darmour's face. The blow snapped his head back and blood sprayed from his nose as he rolled over onto his back. The soldier ran forward and stamped down on him as Darmour raised his arms in attempt to shield himself from the blow. He forced the soldier's leg back and quickly scrambled to his feet, panting heavily, his face bloodied.

"That all you have?" Darmour demanded. "A few sucker blows when a one-handed man's back is turned to you?" He grinned a red, toothy smile.

Was he actually enjoying himself?

Darmour readied himself to go again. This time he did not wait for the strikes to land on him. He charged at one of the soldiers, grabbing hold of a fist full of brown hair at the back of his head before bringing his forearm into the soldier's face multiple times with surprising speed. He only let go when the other soldier attacked him from behind. As Darmour released his hand, Morvin noticed it was filled with hair, and the soldier fell to the floor unconscious.

Darmour threw his head backwards into the remaining soldier's face, each blow being met with a cheer from the crowd. He pulled down the man's arm and stepped out of the grapple, keeping hold of his wrist and stretching his arm out wide. In a blur, he stepped into the soldier and brought down his elbow into his outstretched arm. With a sickening crunch, the man's arm bent the wrong way, and he let out a howl of pain.

Darmour pulled the man's arm forcefully. With a pop, he removed it from its socket to yet an even louder scream from the soldier. Morvin noticed the other members of the group were smiling and Morvin joined them, wondering how brutal Darmour would have been with both his hands and eyes intact. He realised that he had never seen Darmour fight until now.

Darmour pulled backwards, using his weight to spin and hurl the injured soldier straight into the crowd where he went crashing into Captain Reve.

The crowd cheered but quickly quietened when they realised who was underneath the soldier. Judging by the grin on Darmour's, face he had known exactly what he was doing.

"Get him off me!" Reve shrieked as soldiers quickly mobilised to pull him up from the ground. His hair was dishevelled and dusted with sand, and his cheeks burned scarlet.

Even Xerij stood with a rare smile on her face from watching the exchange.

"You think you're funny?" Reve snarled, pulling four different men forward and stepping into the ring himself.

Darmour smiled and simply raised his arms, ready for another round. Morvin's heart sank. Darmour would surely struggle against five people on his own. Anyone would, no matter their strength.

There was a disturbance in the crowd as Zerina knocked soldiers out of her way and raced to Darmour's side.

"Would you look at that? How sweet," Reve taunted. "Very well. If you want a beating as well."

Morvin saw a darkness in Zerina's eyes, one that he had not witnessed before. It was as if the whites of her eyes had turned black. Through the crowd, Vorax stepped forward and stood beside Zerina, followed by Skyrar and Tarin.

"You dare show such petulance?" Reve spat, his face now turning a purplish colour.

"We merely ask that if there was to be a fight, that it remained fair," Tarin answered. "Now it's five against five." The crowd cheered in agreement with Tarin's words, much to the anger of Reve.

Morvin desperately wanted to join them. He stepped forward, but forced himself to stop. This would not help him gain the favour he needed to fulfil his plan. Reluctantly, he stepped back into the crowd. Tarin had instructed them to keep a low profile, and this was the opposite of that. Furthermore, Morvin understood that Captain Reeve was a dangerous man, especially when antagonised. He did not want to give the pompous prick a reason to single him out in retaliation. Celebrating this win with his friends would likely do that. As much as he wanted to, he needed to keep away from them for the time being, even though this isolated him even further.

The soldiers beside Reve eyed up the group with varying levels of alarm, their focus mainly on Vorax who stood far taller than everyone else. On his own, Darmour would have put up a good fight, but collectively, Morvin could not see any outcome other than victory for his friends.

"You want five against five? So be it." Reve reached down and removed his sword from its sheath, holding it in front of him. The crowd's cheers and jeers stopped in an instant, replace with a tense, uncertain silence. The tension between the two groups was storm-like, their focused stares fixed on one another, each with their fists raised with only Reve bearing a weapon.

"That's enough!" Xerij shouted, stepping into the middle of the two groups with her arms outstretched. "I think we have all seen enough for today. It is quite clear that Darmour can fight. He has more than proven himself. I do not want any more soldiers injured. Remember our command from the general, Reve?"

Reve stood silently, glaring at Xerij. Morvin wondered if he would strike her for challenging him in front of everyone. "Very well," he said, re-sheathing his blade. "Do not think this is the end of this. It takes a foolish man to challenge a captain. Your group will not always be by your side," he warned.

Morvin was unsure who his veiled threat was aimed at. Even with his best men, Morvin did not see a situation where Reve would come out on top. The angry captain turned and marched off by himself, vanishing out of sight.

"Everyone, back to your posts!" Xerij barked. "Get those three men to the healers." The injured soldiers were either picked up or dragged away by their arms or feet. Just as quickly, the crowd dispersed, the excitement over for the day. A few soldiers walked up to Darmour and patted him on the back in acceptance. Zerina gave him a tight hug, which Darmour returned with one arm, wincing from his bruised ribs.

"That was a foolish thing to do, Tarin," Xerij warned him as he too patted Darmour on the back with a smile on his face. "Reve is not an enemy you want to have."

"I appreciate your warning, but I would never leave any of my group in an unfair position. I do not care the rank, nor the consequences."

"There is a fine line between bravery and stupidity," Xerij pointed out. "Make sure you are on the right side of it." She nodded, than left them there.

Morvin avoided the temptation to go over to them. He didn't want to be seen with the troublemakers, for risk of jeopardising his position. Instead he remained in the crowd, close enough to watch and listen. He simply nodded and smiled when the group caught him watching from the now-thinned crowd.

Tarin gave him a nod and walked towards him, but when he reached him, he continued past, as if he understood Morvin's strategy.

"I meet my contact tonight," Tarin said in a hushed voice as he walked by without making eye contact. "He left a marker."

Before Morvin had time to reply, Tarin was already past him and circling back to the others.

With this, Morvin turned and headed back to his quarters. For one evening at least, his spirits were lifted. Hopefully he wouldn't have to shovel shit for much longer.

17

"My lord, we have a report." General Precian bowed as he approached King Athos Almerion. The king was sitting at a table making his way through a bowl of fruit that had been served to him skinned and chopped up. Some of the juices ran into his thick, coarse beard. When he saw the general approach, the king rolled his eyes and lowered the sliced apple that sat on a knife in his hand.

"What is it?" he sighed. "I hope it is news of our advancement on Ashula. It has been weeks since you requested reinforcements."

"Reinforcements have been trickling in since I sent conscription letters out across Levanthria." General Precian raised a closed fist to his chest to greet the king, aware of his displeasure of him disturbing his breakfast. "With it brings some problems," he added.

The king sucked his teeth and used his tongue to remove a piece of apple skin that had become wedged between his upper front teeth. "Go on," he said, examining his fingernails with disinterest.

148

"Some of these new arrivals are not of our usual standards. With that, there has come a certain level of disobedience amongst some ranks during preparation of us leaving Kesheria and advancing on Ashula. Captain Reve tells me of a group who are causing him difficulty. He says they have undermined his authority, along with Captain Xerij."

The king slammed his knife into the table, forcing it into the wood. "And you expect me to get involved with such trivial things?" he snapped. "Are we really in a position where our captains cannot regain order amongst my soldiers? Maybe Reve needs replacing. Then again, he is only in his position because his father saved my life on the battlefield. Tell him he has permission to do whatever he feels fit to regain control over this group. We need discipline amongst our ranks, especially at this crucial time in the war. If your plan works, then this war will be over soon, and we will be reunited with our kin in Levanthria." Athos paused for a moment. "Imagine the adulation I would return to. The banners that would line the streets, the pomp and ceremony that would ensue as I give out land to my higher-ranking officers who have fought for so many years. When we are home, I am going to organise the biggest feast that Levanthria has ever seen, and I will go down in history as Levanthria's greatest ruler." He smiled to himself, as if he were the only one present in the room.

"Are you sure, my lord?" General Precian asked. "Captain Reve, he is a bit of a wild one. He doesn't have the respect of the soldiers, unlike the other captains. He uses his rank to solicit favours, to do what he wants."

"Are you questioning my judgement, Precian?" King Athos scoffed. "To solicit control over such a group, you need to display your power from time to time. Do you not agree?"

General Precian dropped his head. "I do, my lord, it's just, I am concerned for the extremes that Captain Reve may take things."

"It is my order. He is a captain in my ranks, and we cannot be seen to be lacking control. You know what will happen if we do not keep control of our soldiers. Now, see to it that word is passed on. You there!"

The king snapped his fingers as a dishevelled and scrawny older man shuffled past the doorway. He wore the king's colours, but he was a face that the king did not recognise. The man had a look of shock about him as he looked around to double-check it was he who the king was addressing. When he realised it was him, he stepped into the king's chamber.

"That's close enough," Athos snapped, curling his nose at the smell of the man.

"I want you to stop what you are doing and go straight back to Captain Reve. You know of him, don't you?"

"Yes – yes, my lord," the man stammered.

"Tell him that the king has given him authority to do what he must to regain control over the camp. Tell him he can make an example of one person." King Athos smiled at General Precian, as if this were a game. "Go!" he barked. "And take this." He grabbed some parchment and scribbled down further instructions, then signed it.

The old man bobbed his head. "Yes, my lord," he said as he exited in a hurry.

"Anything else, General?" the king asked dismissively.

"No, my lord."

"Then I suggest you be on your way. Don't you have a battle plan to draw up? The sooner we are out of this shit hole, the better."

General Precian knew how flippant and rude the king

was, how abhorrent he could be when he lost his temper or became frustrated. How he treated his subjects when they displeased him. His fists clenched tightly behind his back, out of sight of the king.

"My lord," he said, swallowing the bile that he wanted to spew, choking back the words he so desperately wished he could say. He bowed his head and exited out of the king's chamber, following the stone corridor to the battle room where he had his maps and plans laid out. He knew by the way that King Athos had acted that he no longer had his trust. He sent a soldier whose job it was to clean the shit from the latrines to give word to Reve, rather than trusting Precian to deliver the order himself.

If the general had been tasked with delivering the message, he would have toned down the king's orders. King Athos, it seemed, had suspected as much. Precian dreaded to think what Reve would do to make an example of anyone who had disobeyed him. The man was a pompous arse. In fact, the only other person Precian knew of who was as entitled as Reve was King Athos himself.

Precian cursed under his breath. Was it a coincidence that just as the mercenaries he had conscripted arrived that Reve was complaining of disorder? His own orders to Tarin had been for the group to keep their heads down, for them to get on with their postings until he created an opportunity for them to join him in the castle.

Precian knew that he had to be even more careful with communications now. He couldn't be seen singling them out for conversation, or people would become suspicious. If anyone discovered their plans, he would be executed on the spot, his head put on a pike for all to see as a warning for others.

He had been working on this for too long to risk jeopardising it now. It had taken him the last three years – ever since the Battle of Red Cragg – to coordinate his efforts with Tarin, to ensure that the mage would be able to bring the right people into the camp to see out their plan.

Precian picked up a nearby chair and roared as he threw it against the wall. The chair disintegrated on impact, sending splinters of wood across the stone floor. The noise echoed loudly, as did his shouts, but in his flash of anger, he did not care if the king heard him. The king knew what he was doing. He had made threats to harm Precian's family if his next battle plan did not work. The longer they were stuck here, the more impatient King Athos would become. It was a pattern of behaviour that the general was used to, and the last thing he wanted was to see their forces recklessly sacrifices the way they had been in the Battle of Red Cragg. So many lives had been needlessly lost that day, despite Precian's warnings to the king. But Athos had grown bored, paranoid, and reckless. A dangerous combination. General Precian had promised himself that nothing like Red Cragg would ever happen again if he could help it.

He knew that the one thing keeping him safe was the control and respect he had from the king's soldiers. He had led them into battle time and time again, fought alongside them on the front lines. He had killed so many, spilled so much blood, all in the name of King Athos Almerion. They had invaded a land who had sought only to defend themselves from a foreign invader. In fact, Precian held some admiration for the Zarubians and their stubborn reluctance to bend the knee. They had proven a far more difficult enemy than the king had expected.

Unfortunately, the king himself seemed to be negligent in his own memory, for Precian had personally warned him that to invade this land, too fight on terrain his soldiers were not used to, would potentially lead to a long, drawn-out war. It infuriated him even further that the king was now blaming him for the length of time they had been at the keep, unable to push forward.

As far as Precian could see, they were faced with two options. With the reinforcements, they could press ahead with the plan and take the lands east of Ashula, which would put them in a position to advance on the capital and conquer these lands.

Or they could assassinate the king and put an end to the Almerion line. As Athos had no heir, Precian would be able to call on a truce with Zarubia and finally return to Levanthria. The latter would lead to far less bloodshed, with more men and women returning to their families after such a long time.

It was the better option – but for it to work, there needed to be no evidence of Precian's involvement with the plot to kill the king, for if they failed, he and his entire family would be executed.

Precian just needed to find a way to escalate the plan, to get Tarin and his mercenaries on the inside. The only way to do this was to head into camp, but he needed to do this in a way that would not draw attention to him. He had been keeping a close eye on Tarin since he had arrived with his group.

Now it was time to meet Tarin face-to-face. They were running out of time, and they needed to move forward with their plan before it was too late.

Precian slammed his hands on the battle table and looked over the map, letting out an exasperated sigh. In the morning, he would head into camp and use it as an opportunity to meet the soldiers and raise morale. He would look for Tarin and pass word to him of the need to escalate the plan as soon as possible, before the king's impatience destroyed everything he and the mage had been working towards.

18

Not feeling the need to sleep, Morvin spent his night tinkering with Herelda. He received some quizzical looks from soldiers that passed by, but to anyone who asked, he merely told them it was the equivalent of a Dwarven crossbow, which they accepted. By morning time, he had tightened the rivets and the handle, even tinkered with the trigger that connected to the flint, and overall, he was happy with it. It was such a shame that he had nowhere to practice with it.

Morvin smiled as he strapped it to his back. Now that people were noticing it more, he didn't want to leave it unattended just in case someone took a fancy to it.

Following Darmour's brawl and the standoff between their group and Captain Reve, Morvin found his spirits lifted and his motivation to work had increased. Not that he looked forward to his day of shovelling shit, but he did feel as though he had a bit more of a spring in his step. He even found himself whistling a tune as he headed over to the toilets to begin his day, shuddering when he realised what he was doing. Was he turning into Cork?

As he made his way past the sleeping quarters for the other shit tippers, he noticed the very man sat in the far side of the tent. He was rocking back and forth, his head held in his hands.

"Cork?" Morvin stepped inside the tent. No one else was around, and it wasn't like Cork to be the last one to get to work.

Cork didn't acknowledge him. He just continued to rock, his face covered by his scrawny, meatless arms.

"Cork!" Morvin said sternly.

Cork lowered his hands, his face gaunt as if he had not slept through the night either. He didn't have the constitution of a Dwarf, though, nor the ability to go days without sleep.

"What have I done?" Cork said, his face red and blotching, his throat cracked as if he had been in tears for hours.

"Have I missed something?" Morvin asked. "Surely it isn't that bad, Cork. Whatever it is, I am sure we can resolve it." He placed his hand on the old man's shoulder in an attempt to comfort him.

Cork seemed to stare straight through him, a vague blankness in his eyes that was most uncharacteristic of the merry man Morvin had come to know.

"I didn't have a choice. It was an order from the king." Cork raised his trembling hands to his face once more, hiding himself from his shame.

It was at this moment that Morvin noticed the blood stains on Cork's hands.

"What have you done, Cork?"

Cork lowered his hands again, unable to look Morvin in the eyes. His words seemed to be lodged in his throat.

"He made me. Reve, he made me do it."

"What have you done, Cork?" Morvin bellowed. A horrible, sinking feeling in the pits of his stomach began to churn like butter.

"CORK!"

"I'm sorry, Morvin." Cork began sobbing uncontrollably as Morvin spun around and exited the tent, feeling his panic rising.

He could hear the raised groans of soldiers in the main camp. Morvin followed the sound, his brisk walk turning into a run as he rushed to see what the commotion was about. Soldiers were gathering en masse where the brawl had taken place the day before. Morvin barged into the legs of the soldiers on the outer edge of the crowd as he pushed his way through the bodies. His heart banged like a battle drum and his chest heaved as he unapologetically shoved through the crowd.

Horror came over him when he saw what was on full display for everyone to see. A wooden pole had been buried into the ground, and a figure was bound to it.

The figure's clothes had been torn from his body, and his head bobbed down as if he looked at the ground. His skin was flayed from his bones and draped down from his chest, hanging down his legs like a snake shedding its skin. A pool of his blood soaked the sand beneath his mutilated body. The man's face was swollen almost beyond recognition.

But Morvin had sailed with Tarin long enough to recognise him even in such a state.

"No," Morvin cried. "No, no, no!" His ability to walk left him as he dropped to his knees. Tarin was the person who had brought their group together. He was their leader, he was the one with the plans. They were all here in this camp because of him.

Morvin wanted the sand to swallow him into the

ground. The hushed words around him became muffled as he found himself focusing on the blood that slowly dripped from the tip of Tarin's toes.

It was only when he raised his head that he saw a smiling Reve standing beside him, his arms folded and a smug expression on his face.

"Why?" Morvin begged. "Why have you done this?"

"For order," Captain Reve said, stepping forward. "Now that I have your attention, let this serve as a reminder of what happens to those that do not obey the command of your captains."

The crowd tutted and shook their heads in disgust at what they were bearing witness to.

"How did this man disobey you? He didn't!" a voice bellowed from the crowd.

"Yeah!" others followed in protest.

"This man, if you can call him that, directly challenged a captain yesterday. We cannot allow such things to go without punishment. To do so is an act of treason and will be dealt with accordingly." Reve looked at Morvin dead in the eye, knowing that he and Tarin had been friends. He gave Morvin a dark smile that made the Dwarf want to stand up and bash his head in right there and then. But he knew that was not what Tarin would have wanted.

"What is going on here?" A strongly built man walked past Morvin, his voice powerful and commanding.

"General Precian." Captain Reve bowed his head, raising his fist to his chest. "Keeping order, as the king requested."

The general did not look pleased.

"This man and his mercenaries were getting a little unruly. The king tasked me with regaining order when I raised my concerns with you, did he not?"

The general looked up at Tarin's mutilated body for longer than Morvin thought he would have.

"Where is this group now?" the general demanded.

Reve looked around the crowd before raising his hand to point at Morvin. "One of them is here."

Morvin, who had remained on his knees, looked up at the general as the man stepped towards him and pummelled his face.

Morvin's vision exploded with a flash of light. The general's strength was far stronger than what he would have imagined.

"Then we shall make an example of him too!" The general grabbed a tight fistful of Morvin's hair and dragged him backwards. Morvin didn't fight back. His limbs felt as though they didn't belong to him. In a blurred daze, he saw the saddened faces of Skyrar and Vorax, who looked ready to fight. He raised his hand to stop them. Whatever the general had planned for him, they couldn't react. They had come too far, were too close. All they needed was to get Morvin's powder inside. Morvin didn't know if Tarin had even managed this. All he knew was that his chances of being put on keep duty were disintegrating faster than a falling star.

"Are there any others?" the general demanded. "CAPTAIN! I was told there was a group of people causing you trouble." The general looked at Tarin's body once more and seemed to hesitate for a moment, as if lost in his own thoughts. When he turned to face Morvin, Morvin could see that he was enraged.

"But the king's order was to make an example of one of them," Captain Reve protested.

"I am in charge here," General Precian snarled. For a

moment, Morvin thought the general was about to step towards the captain and strike him.

Captain Reve frantically scanned the crowd until his eyes fell on Vorax and Skyrar. "Over there," he stammered, "and there." He pointed a finger to Zerina standing a few steps away from Skyrar. Her face was streaming with tears. Darmour was beside her, his arms wrapped around her shoulders. "And him, he has been the catalyst for all of this."

There was no sign of Ulrik. Morvin had no idea if the pirate captain was even associated with the rest of the group, given how elusive he had been since their arrival.

"Seize them," the general ordered.

Soldiers sprang into action, apprehending each member of the group. Morvin wondered why Zerina didn't simply use her magic, but when he looked over at her, he could see that she stood slumped and unconscious. Only the soldiers' grips prevented her from falling to the ground.

It was a testament to their shock at Tarin's death that no one really fought back.

"Where are you taking them?" Captain Reve demanded as he scurried alongside the stony-faced general.

"To the stocks in the keep!" the general growled. "You want a reminder for those who do not follow your lead? Let this help you in your quest. I am sure a few days in the stocks without food or water will help."

Morvin's legs trailed behind him as he was dragged through the sand by his hair all the way up to the fort and through the entrance of the keep. They finally stopped in front of some stocks which stood buried in the sand.

Morvin was released, and his head bounced off the ground, causing his vision to shake.

"Stand!" the general commanded.

In a daze and ready to let himself drift into the darkness, Morvin was barely able to do as he was told. When he did, the general raised the wooden bar on top of the stocks and said, "Place your head and arms across." He looked over at Reve who stood just a few metres away. "Now, unless you want me to make an example of the rest of your group!" he bellowed, much to the joy of Captain Reve.

Reluctantly, Morvin stepped forward, his matted hair clinging to his sweaty face as he placed himself in the stocks from a standing position.

The general slammed down the top of the stocks, a tight pressure forcing its way down on Morvin's breath, restricting his breathing enough to make it incredibly uncomfortable for him. He had a thicker neck than the average man that this device was designed for.

As the general began tightening the clasps, he muttered, "I am sorry for your loss."

Morvin was taken aback by his sudden change in tone. For a moment he thought the blow to the face had caused him to confuse General Precian's words.

"And I apologise for what I must do, to you and the rest of your group. It was the only way I could get close to you without causing alarm. Tarin was a good man."

In an instant, Morvin realised that General Precian was the informant that Tarin had spoken of, the man who he had been plotting with all this time.

"Don't say anything," the general continued through hushed breath as he locked the stock into place. "Where is the powder that Tarin sent word of?"

Morvin didn't know if he could trust the general, but at this stage, he did not have much option.

"It's in the barrels we brought. It is hidden under a glamour under the bottles of ale and rice."

"I am sorry for what you must endure now, sorry for Tarin. It is the only way that I can draw no suspicion to you or I. You can trust me, I am an ally."

Morvin could be forgiven for questioning if fact he was dreaming, the conversation from the general seemed so surreal.

In his periphery, he could see the others being locked up as well.

General Precian walked away from Morvin and turned towards Reve. "Captain, let this serve as a further warning to the soldiers under your command," he bellowed so that as many soldiers that were watching on could hear. "Anyone choosing to oppose or disobey commands will face consequences like this group here. I'd say three days ought to show them what associating with the wrong people does for you. As for the rest of your soldiers, they also need to learn. Fetch every bottle of ale or spirit. When you and the other captains are confident that you have regained order, I may release it back to your ranks."

"Yes, General." Reve saluted him.

"And Captain?" the general followed up whilst turning away.

"Yes?"

"Do not let this disorder fall upon your ranks again."

"Yes, General,"

"Consider me displeased. Ensure these are all on display for the rest of the soldiers to see. Make sure there is sufficient distance between the stocks. We don't want them communicating with one another while they are here." Then the general walked back into the keep, leaving Morvin and the others in the stocks like trophies on display in a great hall.

He did not even give the Dwarf a second glance.

Morvin's mind raced as he tried to come to terms with everything that had just happened. Tarin was gone. And now Morvin and his friends were going to have to endure three days of torture, during which he would have to dig deeper than ever before.

But out of nowhere, their plan had progressed. Morvin now knew the informant. He now knew there was a way to put the powder into place. He was dazed, in pain, and hurting from the loss of Tarin, but somehow, the sneaky bastard had gotten the general of the king's army on their side.

19

Morvin's head felt like a storm was brewing inside. His body ached, and his mind felt as though it had become nothing more than a pool of pulp since his punishment had started. He had little to no room to move aside from rotating his blistered wrists. His neck had become numb from the pressure, having only stared at his feet since he had been here, unable to turn and see the others. Just like them, he had remained silent all this time, but surely they did not have much longer. Surely they would be released soon, and he would be able to update everyone on Tarin's contact, General Precian.

For three long days Morvin stood, his head bowed towards the sandy terrain, his hands hanging loosely from either side of his head in the stocks. The general was right; it had been a torturous three days. His stomach growled in starvation, his mouth drier than the barren Mouth of Antar in Levanthria. He found it difficult to swallow, not only because of the constriction around his neck but also from the swelling of his throat and tongue through dehydration.

He didn't know which was the worst part: the starvation, the agony in his arms and legs, or being left to nothing but his own thoughts for this entire time.

As he stared into the sand, his mind became fragmented, nearing the point of being unable to go on any longer. His 'punishment' for being associated with Tarin.

Every minute felt like a lifetime. Each second, Morvin revisited the vision of seeing Tarin's mangled corpse tethered to a wooden post. His only crime had been standing up to a snivelling coward of a captain. Morvin vowed to avenge his fallen friend. The one thing that kept him going, stopped him breaking his mind, was the knowledge that the others endured what he did. In silence they supported one another, even if he could not see them. Only Ulrik had evaded this torture, wherever he was.

For Morvin, the question now was who would meet his fury first: the king, or Captain Reve. By hook or by crook, he would make Captain Reve pay for what he had done. He could only imagine the agony that Tarin had faced in his final moments, to have his skin torn from him. Morvin could only hope that by this time, Tarin was already at peace in the afterlife. He had not deserved what had happened to him. He was a good man who had only wanted what was best for Levanthria. The fact that the king had ordered this simply served to motivate Morvin further, to make the endurance of this pain and suffering more bearable. The knowledge that Reve had acted on the king's command only solidified that he was a tyrant, one that needed to be stopped at all costs before he could infest these lands any further. Only then would Levanthria bring a sigh of relief, only then could they bring a new age of prosperity over the lands.

Muffled footsteps drew upon Morvin and the pressure around his neck lifted as the stock was raised.

His legs gave from underneath him, and he crumpled in a heap on the sand, the warmth of the sun searing into him. His skin felt as though it were on fire.

"Here." General Precian knelt and poured some water from a flask into his mouth. "Consider your time spent," he said. "Know that I will need your help to get the powder inside. The key is for it to be undetected. There are small tunnels that connect to the toilets, to drains outside of the keep. I believe you empty the excrements of the soldiers into one of the pits, yes? I suggest you use this as your opportunity to get inside. We will only have one opportunity for this."

The general stood up. "I suggest you recover and ready your men. When the opportunity presents itself, I will light a blue flame in the window of the eastern walls. Do you understand?"

"Yes," Morvin croaked, dazed from thirst and hunger. He hadn't spoken a word for three days. His tongue was swollen and his skin burned in agony from prolonged exposure to the harsh sun.

"Take them back to camp," the general commanded. Morvin was scooped up by two soldiers, an arm over either one. They bore the brunt of his weight as his feet did not touch the ground. He looked to his right and could see Darmour, Zerina, Skyrar, and Vorax being freed from the stocks and limply dragged away by the guards.

Morvin's head bobbed and lulled as the camp drew closer. Eyes cast shame upon him as the other soldiers looked on with varying shades of disgust.

"Thanks to you lot, we have had no ale!" one voice spat, although Morvin did not see whose voice it was. His head was simply too heavy to lift as he was carried through the camp.

"This place was only bearable when we could drink, scum," another man spat.

"I would sleep with one eye open if I were you, Dwarf," one of the soldiers carrying him said. "There is a lot of anger towards you and your group since the other day. Safe to say you are more vulnerable than the rest of them though."

Morvin found himself driving in and out of consciousness as his shoulders sagged above him. His entire body throbbed in agony, but he found the energy to muster a smile under his breath. He would do as the general had said, he would do what Tarin had always said. He would bide his time and through that patience, he would find the right moment. He would get his revenge. For his wife, for his son, for Tarin, for every person who had lost their life in this god-forsaken war.

When he reached the familiar surroundings of his quarters, the soldiers dumped him on the ground by some sheets that Morvin recognised as his own. They were filthy; the other soldiers had defecated and urinated on them.

Morvin scrambled to his knees, pushing sand over the top until the sheet was buried. Then, with an aching body, he rolled onto his back and let out an almighty groan before lying in silence. A strange, whooshing noise raced through his head in time with his heartbeat. His arms were heavy, his energy sapped. But his motivation, that he felt rising. His spirit, although low, was not broken entirely, even if it was only the thinnest piece of threaded resolve that kept him from shattering into a million pieces.

He was too close now. He didn't have much further to go. All he needed to do now was let his body recover, use the time that was on his side. And within that, he knew he would find his moment.

"Here, I have food and water for you," came Cork's cracked voice. His words were spoken cautiously, and rightfully so. For if Morvin had the energy or the ability, he would gladly end him for being complicit in Tarin's death.

Morvin looked at the scrawny old man with strained eyes, his hatred for him burning into him more harshly than the sun. Cork ignored this and propped Morvin's head up before tipping his own flask of water into his mouth.

Morvin coughed and spluttered as his mouth absorbed with water, pouring from his mouth as if he were drowning. He found that he could slowly move his tongue as the water cleansed his dehydration. It wasn't as comforting or as refreshing as Morvin had anticipated.

He tried to raise his arms to snatch the flask and drink for himself. He didn't want to accept help from someone who had assisted in the flaying of Tarin. As he grabbed hold of the flask from Cork, his hands trembled wildly, and he spilled the water over his face, barely managing to get any into his mouth.

Mumbled noises continued to leave his mouth until he eventually found the ability to form a word. "Go!" he growled, his throat hoarse.

"I am sorry, Morvin, I didn't have a choice," Cork protested. His frail body looked as though it may fail him. His face was pale and his eyes puffy, his skin almost translucent as it hung from him.

"We always have a choice," Morvin heaved as bile rose from his belly. The rage within was as though he were about to spew fire over Cork. "Go!" he demanded. "Next time you look one of us in the eyes, know the pain you have caused, know that you walk here freely because you aided in torturing our friend, my friend."

Cork lowered his head in shame, his eyes drifting over

the dirt underfoot. "Very well," he said quietly, his voice awash with guilt.

"I think he told you to leave," Skyrar scolded from the entranceway of the tent. She was accompanied by Darmour, Vorax, and Zerina. Vorax's frame cast a heavy shadow over her, her face hidden as she bowed her head.

Cork scurried to leave, turning slightly and pressing himself between Darmour and Vorax who both stood as if they were debt collectors, their arms crossed in front of them.

When Cork left, Zerina pushed into the tent. "Keep a look out? We can't afford them to see my magic." She knelt by Morvin and placed her hands on his chest, then began to mutter incoherent words under her breath. Her hands started to glow with a flash of white as her magic pulsated into Morvin. Slowly, his body started to ache less.

"I can soothe the pain as best I can, but I cannot heal you fully. To do so would only draw more attention on you. Captain Reve has forbidden the healers from coming to help us. Little does he know, I have magic. I have already done the same with the others."

Morvin understood and appreciated Zerina's help as the rhythmic pulse washed over him, wave after wave.

"Th – thank you," Morvin said, finding that his jawline ached less and the swelling of his tongue had reduced.

When Zerina stepped away, Morvin found he was able to shuffle himself up into a sitting position and drink more freely from the flask, albeit with his hands still trembling. As he did so, he noticed the protruding, black veins creeping up the backs of Zerina's hands like cracks in granite. She pulled her flask from her side and took a drink, and as she did so, the blackened veins stopped progressing and ran back down to her fingertips before vanishing.

"What is that?" Morvin asked.

"Think of it as a tonic," Zerina said. "It helps me with my magic use, stops it destroying my body."

"If the king knew about that?" Morvin said. "Imagine what he could do with his mages if he had that potion."

"It comes at too high of a price," Zerina spoke in a saddened tone, her eyes becoming vacant as if her thoughts went elsewhere. "And we are not here to aid the king."

Skyrar had remained stood in the doorway watching on, but now she stepped into the tent, revealing her bloodied and bruised face.

"What in the shit happened to you?" Morvin asked.

"You should have seen the other three that jumped me." She grinned. It was in this moment that he saw Zerina also smarted a bruised cheek. Darmour was black and blue and even Vorax smarted a bust lip.

"You should keep the look." Morvin smiled. "It's an improvement."

His words brought a sly smile from Skyrar, a welcome reprieve from her usual cold features.

"Safe to say it has been a rough few days," Darmour said, keeping a steady eye on anyone approaching the tent. "They blame us for losing the booze. Reve has made it his mission to make our lives unpleasant. We cannot stay long. In fact, it is probably best for us to keep our distance after this meeting until we come up with a plan."

"The plan's fucked," Skyrar spat. "I can't believe what they did to Tarin. I swear by the gods that they will pay for what they did to him." Her voice cracked, a rare shot of an emotion other than anger.

"It isn't," Morvin reassured them. "I grieve for our friend. I did not know him as long as you but in that short time, I found that he was a good man, one who only wanted what is best for Levanthria." His tongue stuck to the roof of his mouth as he spoke, so Morvin brought up his flask of water once again to quench his drying mouth. "It is because of him that we are so close, that we are in touching distance into putting our plan into motion." He smiled at the others. "To achieving what Tarin wanted."

"How so?" Vorax asked. Beside her, Darmour leant into the room curiously.

"I know who Tarin was liaising with from the camp. His contact revealed himself to me," he said. "And the best part is that he has told me how we are going to get my powder inside that keep."

Morvin knew that any chance of gaining favour to be on keep duties was long gone, so this was their only shot at succeeding with their mission. "I know how we can get inside, but we are going to need a distraction."

20

"Has order resumed within our ranks?" King Athos Almerion asked as he paced around the war room like a caged animal. His hands were tucked behind his back, and he sighed loudly as General Precian studied the large map on the table.

"Captain Reve assures me that the soldiers are standing back in line, however unorthodox his methods are," the general said, moving a piece of stone farther east on the map of Zarubia.

"Unorthodox?" King Athos asked with a puzzled expression. "He has quickly regained control of the camp, has he not? Something which appears to have been disrupted by the arrival of the reinforcements you requested."

General Precian breathed in slowly, swallowing his anger towards the king. He chose instead to focus on the map as he finalised the battle plan.

They were close, so desperately close. They had the powder, they had the person who could activate it and a way of making the assassination look as though it was the work of magic. All he needed was for the Dwarf to follow the advice General Precian had given him and make his way inside the keep, kill the King, and allow him to end this god-forsaken war.

"How long until we advance?" the king demanded. "How long until we leave this wretched place?"

"The soldiers are nearing ready, my lord," the general started. "We are just waiting on the final battalion of soldiers to arrive."

"What about the mages?" Athos asked. "How many do we have remaining in our ranks? How many has Morgana been able to train?"

The name sent a chill down General Precian's spine, her name causing his blood to run cold. He had never had the displeasure of meeting the sorceress, but he had been told in graphic detail the kind of things that she had done, not only in the dungeons of Askela but in plain sight for all to see. Things the king had given her permission to do, all in his desperate attempt to win a war that he had started for his own gain.

"So far there have been around fifteen mages that have arrived with the reinforcements. Their training is as best as can be given the rushed nature of their deployment. The sorceress herself sent letter to confirm that she was not finished with them, but understood the need of their hasty arrival."

The king smiled antagonistically. "You really do not like to speak her name, do you, General?" He shuffled one of the pieces on the map towards the eastern territories of Zarubia. "Why is that?"

"You know I do not approve of her methods, nor her magic."

"Remember who you are speaking to, General," the king

said calmly. "It is thanks to Morgana that we have been able to advance to this point. Without her quick intervention, we would not have had access to the magic that has helped us to hold the line."

General Precian could not help but wonder why the witch hadn't come here to fight herself if she was that good.

"Now, when are we advancing? I am through being kept here," the king diverted, staring into the general's eyes.

"As I said, we should be ready in another few days." Precian hoped this would give the Dwarf enough time to enact their plan.

"Make it sooner. I have received word that the Zarubians are planning an attack," the king said nonchalantly, as if passing on unimportant information.

General Precian's heart sank. It was as if the king sought to tease him, as if he knew that he was plotting something. Precian banished the thought as quickly as it entered his mind, putting it down to paranoia. If Athos had the slightest inkling of the general's plot to take his life, he would have been exposed to a punishment far worse than the flaying that Tarin had endured.

"You have received information? Where from? And why am I only just hearing about it?" All military communication came through the general.

"Don't concern yourself with where the information has come from. I believe it to be true and I have already thought of a plan."

"My lord, do you question the methods I employ to keep you safe? After all these years, it is all I have strived to do. The things I have done to keep you safe and win the war..."

The king smiled as he sat down on the opposite side of the table and pored over the map. "Relax, General Precian. I have already warned what will happen if you fail me. But remember that out of the two things you just listed, there is only one which you have been successful with. You have one more day to put this plan of yours into action and it better be more effective than Red Cragg."

General Precian felt the hair on his arms rise, and his arms shook as he leant on the table. The fact that the king blamed him for the battle plan at Red Cragg was insulting. It would have worked had the king followed through with the general's command. But he hadn't, all because he hadn't wanted to risk losing too many damned mages.

Either side of the Red Cragg was hemmed in by the large rock formations on either side, rendering anyone passing through a sitting duck. In not sending the extra soldiers to aid those trapped there, it meant that on that dark day, they lost more soldiers in that battle than the rest of the war combined. So many were sent to their deaths for no reason, with them losing ground on top of it. It was what had caused them to flee to this keep and set up defences, a place that, aside from the odd scout attack, had been relatively easy to defend.

The fact that the king was speaking to Precian as though it were his actions that had sent all those souls to the afterlife only confirmed just how far removed the king was from this war and from his people.

"My plan will work, my lord," the general said. He wasn't lying; he was confident that his plan would work. Just not the one the king was thinking about.

"Either way, we prepare to leave in one day," said King Athos, "before those Zarubians have time to 'ambush' us."

"How can you be sure – "

Athos simply smiled and nodded his head. "I am sure."

"But my lord, if you give me just a little longer, I can

ensure every soldier is how they should be, we will be as best prepared as possible."

"If they are not ready by tomorrow, what difference will an extra day make? You have one day, General."

A day did not give Precian the time he needed to ensure the others were ready. The Dwarf and his partners had only just been released from the stocks and likely would need at least couple of days to recover. If they were going to succeed with their plan, it needed to happen tonight. They needed to act now. Why did Athos have to be so impulsive? Why, when they had been here so long, had he decided they had to progress with the plan the next day, when he was so close?

"Is there something which you want to say to me?" the king asked. "Something you wish to get from your chest?"

"No, my lord. Your soldiers will be ready by morning." Precian swallowed, his mind racing with his different options. He could kill the king right here, right now, in this very room. At least then it would be over. He fantasised for a moment about how it would feel to wrap his hands around the king's throat and squeeze the last ebb of life away from him. There were guards outside of the room, however, and if he was to be tried as the person who assassinated the king, it would be a death sentence to those he held dearest across the seas in Levanthria. He would be executed straight away as a king slayer, and the ability to call upon a truce with the Zarubians would be rendered impossible. He needed that Dwarf to enter the keep and he needed him to do it tonight.

"I grow tired," the king said as he stood from his chair and exited the room. "Make sure you are ready. Best send word to your captains. Or is that something you need me to do?" he sniped as he left.

Was that another veiled threat?

The king was acting irrationally, and General Precian did not like it. Wasting no time, he placed one of his lamps in a large stone window frame. Then he took one of the stones from the war table and threw it inside the lamp. Gheylar stone had a strange property – when exposed to flame, it glowed blue in colour. He just hoped it would succeed at drawing the Dwarf's attention to the keep, even though it was earlier than planned.

General Precian quickly made his way down to the entranceway of the keep, the soldiers on guard saluting him as he passed. When he reached the camp, it felt quiet and subdued. There was no raucous laughter. The only soldiers he could see were those who were on patrol and those that were still eating their rations. The soldiers nodded at him and saluted, but the general could tell by their stony expressions that they were not happy to see him.

"Where are the captains?" the general asked a woman who sat slurping soup from a wooden bowl.

She near spat out the soup as if surprised that the general was speaking to her directly. "Towards the mess hall," she said. "They usually eat and drink together at this time."

The general marched through camp, all the while keeping his eyes open for any sign of the Dwarf. Morvin was the only link to the group. He did not know how many mercenaries Tarin had brought overall, and he did not think he would be able to pick out their faces.

The mess hall was towards the healers' tents, and as the general continued to walk through camp, a strange silence hung in the air that only served to increase his apprehension.

When he reached the tent, he could hear raised voices

from inside. He pulled the cloth of the entrance back to see what was going on.

"You did not think with your head, Reve! You let you anger get the better of you. Because of that, three times I have had to stop brawls where soldiers have jumped the mercenaries who arrived with Tarin." Captain Xerij was standing over Captain Reve who sat at a table, a bowl of soup tipped on its side in front of him.

"Are you implying I had something to do with that?" Captain Reve gave Xerij a goading smile which all but confirmed his guilt in the allegations.

"We need the soldiers to be on side with one another," she scolded. "Turning them against one another will only serve to fragment them further. But that isn't what this is about, is it? All this was about was flexing your small dick!"

Reve turned a shade of scarlet as he stood from his chair forcefully, knocking it backwards into the ground.

"I'll show you small dick." He launched himself over the table at Xerij who stood her ground, laughing at him. She was not intimidated by the captain and the general liked that. She had something about her and did not suffer fools.

"What is going on?" the general growled, making his presence known.

Reve stopped in his tracks, lowering his raised fist. Captain Xerij placed her hands behind her and turned to face the general, bowing her head to him.

"General Precian," she said, "I was merely speaking to Captain Reve about his approach with the soldiers."

"Is what Captain Xerij says true? Have you set soldiers upon some of the reinforcements, even after they have already undergone their punishments?"

"It is, General," Reve said without remorse. "They seek to disrupt this camp. I merely wish to keep them all in line.

After all, they are associated with Tarin and the Dwarf." He looked disgusted with the mere mention of the Dwarf.

"Did I not already set a precedent for this by leaving them in the stocks for three days?"

"I sought only to remind them of their place," Captain Reve sneered.

"Remember who it is you address, Captain. Remember how it was that you got your rank," Precian scolded. He could not stand the snivelling coward. Reve had not earned his rank through battle like the other captains. He had got his position through his father who died on the battlefield protecting the king. If only that arrow had missed him and hit the intended target, this war would have been over long ago.

"The king gave you that rank, did he not, because of your father's bravery?"

Captain Reve puffed up his shoulders like he was a petulant child, his cheeks still glowing with a flash of red. "I am a captain of the king's army," he rasped.

"A rank you have received without any battle experience, unlike Captain Xerij here," the general said calmly. He was in a foul mood and perhaps knocking this pompous, spoiled captain on his arse would make him feel better.

"Next time we are on the battlefield, remember that it is these very soldiers who will fight for you. Mistreat them, and you may find a Levanthrian arrow in your back."

"Are you threatening me?" Captain Reve said through gritted teeth. To be fair to him, he did not show any signs of backing down even though it was the general who scolded him. Perhaps in another life, that could have been used to train him into a fine soldier.

"I merely say it to serve as a warning, Reve, for men will not fight alongside you if you persistently mistreat them.

Even the most obedient dog would turn on its master when hungry." The general stepped towards Captain Reve and lifted the collar of his tunic to straighten him out. "In the future when you are in the presence of a general, make sure you are dressed so." He smiled in a patronising way before turning towards Captain Xerij. She wore a sly smile, which told him she had enjoyed witnessing the dressing down.

"That does not mean your actions do not go without consequence," he scolded. Captain Xerij dropped her shoulders as quickly as her smile and bowed her head.

"Now the reason that I am here at this hour," Precian said, placing both his hands calmly behind his back, "is because the king has given orders for you to ready your soldiers for battle. When the morning arrives, we march on Ashula. When that city falls, we will have victory."

"Are we ready for that, General?" Captain Xerij asked. "The reinforcements have not been here long."

"King Athos wants to advance, so we are advancing. It takes a foolish man to go against the will of King Athos Almerion," General Precian said before making to leave the tent. "Have our soldiers ready by the morning. I need to take a piss and finalise the battle plans." With this, the general left.

21

B y the time Morvin had finished telling the rest of the group of General Precian's involvement, his belly had grown even more ravenous. He had not eaten for three days, a feat that was impressive for a human, let alone a Dwarf.

"You are sure the general said that? After all, you did take quite the strike to the face, before you were dragged off. Maybe you were hallucinating?" Skyrar spoke in disbelief.

"How on earth would Tarin have got a general of the king's army onside with our plan? To even risk discussing it likely would end with execution," Darmour added.

The more Morvin though about it, the more he began to doubt it himself. He sounded as though madness had taken over him, a more likely scenario given he had spent three days in the stocks under the intense heat that these lands brought.

"I swear my words are true," Morvin said as if speaking aloud merely served as a way of convincing himself. "I am telling you, the general has told me out to get inside the keep through the drains." He spoke with a growl, part of him frustrated at the group's reluctance to believe him.

"Keep your voice lowered, Morvin," Vorax said, poking her head outside to make sure no one else was around. "We don't want others to hear of our plan."

"Did he tell you when? When are we to act on this plan?" Skyrar asked, helping herself to the rations that Cork had left for Morvin. He scowled at her and snatched the bowl from her. The soup smelled dreadful, like off vegetables had been used. But at this stage, he did not care, and he tipped the bowl back, downing the cold, stale soup in one go. His stomach churned as he feasted for the first time in days. When he was finished, he noticed the others were looking at him intently, waiting for answers.

"He did not tell me when, just to watch out for a blue flame in the window. When we see that, we move."

"Through the drains," Zerina said. "How are we to get to them without being seen? There are soldiers on patrol, constantly round the perimeter and inside the upper walls of the keep."

"We will need a distraction," Morvin said. "There is enough of us to do that, is there not?" He looked around the group. "Where's Ulrik?" he asked, realising that the pirate captain was missing.

"On patrol, I assume," Zerina sighed. "I have not seen him since we got back from the stocks."

"We need to get word to him," Morvin said. "If this plan is going to work, it is going to take all of us. Now, I imagine the drains will not be the biggest, but I was thinking if we separated into two groups, Skyrar will be small enough to enter through the drains with me, which leaves Vorax, Darmour, Zerina, and Ulrik to –"

"Create a distraction," Darmour finished with a sigh.

"Why is it that whenever there needs to be a distraction, it's the bigger ones who get lumbered with the task?"

"Wait, wait, wait," Skyrar protested. "I like how you are presuming I am happy to crawl through shit to get inside. Why can't I create a distraction with the others?"

"We are all going to need to get a little dirty on this night," Zerina said.

"Aye, lass," Morvin said. "The more powder we can move into the keep, the better. Gives us a greater chance of opening the place up. Besides, I need someone who is a master of locks to get us inside the cellar."

Skyrar's face dropped, less than happy with her role. "We should be talking about what to do with Reve," she spat.

"We will avenge Tarin," Morvin promised. "The first opportunity you are left alone with Reve, you do what needs to be done."

"I'll feed the cowardly pig his entrails," she said, her frown turning into a stern smile.

"So, we have the semblance of a plan," said Darmour. "The only question now is deciding when we do it. We are only going to get one chance. Fail or get captured, and that will be it for us."

"As long as we get to the king, as long as I know that he is no longer of this world, I will gladly sail into the afterlife with open arms." Morvin's greatest desire, when all this was done, when they had completed their plan, was to be reunited with his wife and son.

"That settles it then. All that remains is waiting for the opportune moment," Vorax said. Standing by the tent's entrance, she pulled back the doorway to leave.

Morvin looked beyond her. In the distance, the castle keep loomed over these desert plains. It was a view that he had used to inspire him each and every day that he left for his posting, one that he could likely sketch with his eyes shut.

But something was different.

The sun had begun to set for its brief night. In the darkness, a blue light flickered in one of the upper windows, a distant glow that Morvin had not noticed before.

This was it. This was the sign they had been waiting for. Morvin was not expecting it so soon after being released from the stocks with the others. Something must have changed.

Without saying anything, Morvin scrambled to his feet and dashed outside.

"What is it?" Zerina asked.

"The blue flame." Morvin spun back around to face everyone. "The time is now."

He limped to his effects that sat next to his makeshift bed. "I'd be damned if I did this wearing the king's colours." He ripped off his mail armour and tunic, then pulled out the clothes he had arrived in. They were dusty from the sand, but they would do.

"Fuck," Skyrar scolded, turning quickly. "Your bare arse is the last thing I wish to see before we embark on a suicide mission."

"Take it as a good luck charm, lass." Morvin cheekily slapped his bare cheeks and the others laughed. All except Skyrar, whose cheeks turned scarlet. "We need to move now," Morvin said, "before the opportunity is lost."

"Are we really going to dive in and do this now?" Zerina asked. "Do we not need to approach this situation with caution?"

"There is such a thing as over-caution," Darmour said.

"If Morvin here is saying that now is the time, then now is the time. We need to find Ulrik."

"I am sure Ulrik will figure out what is happening when he sees the commotion," Zerina said.

"Darmour, Zerina, Vorax," Morvin started, "take this barrel of powder. Draw attention from the western patrol. That should buy us the time we need. You will need this, too." Morvin reached into his bag and retrieved a flint mechanism, which he tossed to Darmour. "Use it as a last resort to ignite the powder, but know that whoever sparks it in close range will likely not survive the blast. I would suggest using your magic to ignite it from a distance, if possible," he told Zerina.

"Three against an entire army. What could possibly go wrong?" Darmour sighed sarcastically.

"I need the blast to draw all the guards away from the drains at the north of the keep. That way, we can get inside unnoticed."

"Good luck, friends. May the gods look down on you with favour on this night," Vorax said, bowing her head before the two of them left.

"What now?" Skyrar asked, peering over the top of Morvin's shoulder.

"Now, we wait."

22

Darmour's chest heaved as they tentatively made their way through camp with the barrel of powder in Vorax's arms. Even as darkness greeted the camp, the air was still warm. There was no breeze, and his chainmail and tunic only made him more uncomfortable.

"What do you suggest we do?" Vorax said as they pushed through camp suspiciously.

"Look for an opportune moment, I suppose." Darmour shrugged. "What's going on up there?"

A group of soldiers were rushing into each tent, waking the others up.

"Get up!" Darmour heard one of the soldiers call. "We advance on Ashula at dusk. It's the king's orders!"

"Shit," Darmour muttered, realising that if everyone was readying themselves for battle, the window of opportunity was even smaller.

"You two, make sure you are ready," the same soldier barked at Darmour, Vorax, and Zerina as he exited the tent.

"Aye," Darmour said with a growl, nodding.

"Well, there is no time like the present," Vorax huffed, setting down the barrel of powder. As she reached for the axe that was strapped to her back, Darmour raised his hand to stop her.

"What are you doing?" she asked. "We need to create the distraction."

"Come, let's place the powder on the periphery of camp. It doesn't sit well with me causing harm or injury to innocent soldiers," Darmour mused as he gestured for Vorax and Zerina to follow him.

"It's all going to shit!" Vorax said, but she hoisted the barrel of powder back onto her shoulder and fell in step beside Darmour.

"This would explain the blue lamp being placed so soon," said Zerina, following close behind.

They were able to reach the outer edge of the camp easily with the soldiers all buzzing around in a poorly coordinated fashion. There did not seem to be one person taking charge, just hundreds of men and women gathering their weapons and armour to ready themselves for battle. A younger soldier stood in a nearby tent, a ghastly pale colour as the gravity of war seemed to dawn on him. His helmet was poorly fitted, and his tunic drowned him as if it had belonged to a much more rotund soldier before it was his.

"These soldiers don't stand a chance," Vorax said as the three of them navigated the walkways. "Most of these are not warriors."

"Come, place the powder over here."

"Do you still think we need such a distraction? The camp seems pretty distracted to me," Zerina pointed out as they marched away from camp. Vorax placed the barrel down in the sand in a position close enough to draw attention, but far enough from the nearest tents so as to avoid unnecessary harm.

"Aye, but we need to draw the soldiers from the other side of camp to here so that Morvin and Skyrar can get into the keep unnoticed," Darmour replied. "Zerina, do you think you can hit the barrel from over there?" He gestured to the tent where the young soldier had been just moments ago.

The soldier had set off walking in the opposite direction, but then Darmour noticed him pause. A noise in the distance had caught on the passing wind.

Darmour remained hesitant, tilting his head as he listened. A strange sound was growing louder and louder at an alarming rate, crackling like a raging fire. As he looked up at the sky, a ball of fire came hurtling through the air as if white-hot boulders were falling from the stars.

"Run!" Darmour cried, diving into Zerina to shield her.

The two of them knelt low as the fireball crashed down where they had stood seconds before.

The barrel of powder exploded.

The force blew the three of them through the air, and as Darmour gathered himself, all he could hear was a metallic ringing in his ears.

"Zerina!" he groaned. "Vorax!"

Vorax was scrambling to her feet. "Where did that come from?"

"Magic!" Darmour roared. He had seen enough fire magic from Zerina to recognise its power. He climbed up from the ground, and his vision took a few moments to straighten as he took in the smouldering crater that now sat in the sand nearby. Plumes of smoke billowed upwards into the night sky, veiling the stars above in a cloak of shadows. The ground still shook from the explosion, as though the crater in the ground crackled with flames.

"If that didn't get everyone's attention, nothing will," Vorax said.

"Where did it come from though? Where is Zerina?" Darmour frantically searched for her, his heart racing as adrenaline pounded through his body.

"Zarubians!" a soldier's voice cried out. "We're under attack!"

Any soldiers remaining in their tents now hurried outside. Those that were already on patrol took up defensive positions as more balls of fire rained down on the camp. Sand sprayed into the air as flaming bodies of screaming soldiers wandered around before collapsing in heaps on the ground.

Through the chaos, Darmour saw the crumpled form of Zerina. She was slumped on her side and unconscious. "Over there!" he cried.

He and Vorax ran to her at once. When they reached her, Darmour rolled her to face him as terror seized him. Her cheek was burnt, and she had a gash at the top of her head, but she was breathing. Darmour wiped her bloodied hair from her face and stroked her cheek. "I've got you," he said.

Vorax picked her up from the ground with ease and turned to find the soldiers hastily moving into formation just before the smouldering crater.

"Mages!" Darmour heard the voice of Captain Xerij cry. Her voice was hoarse as she screamed out commands. Darmour knew that they were unprepared for an attack like this, at this time. Levanthrian soldiers continued to line up in formation, readying themselves for the surprise invasion. As another wave of fire came down upon them, Levanthrian mages channelled their energies to cast protection spells over the camp. The flaming balls hit invisible barriers in the sky, exploding on impact and spraying molten ash to its sides. The mages strained as they used their magic to protect the others at great cost to themselves. Darmour knew enough of magic to know that it was only a matter of time until the affliction from magic use would set in for them.

"Storm casters, flame wielders, earth shakers!" Captain Xerij roared, her sword stretched into the air. "With me!"

Mages of varying ages and sizes followed Xerij to where the blasts were coming from as the sky above continued to flash with burning flames of magic.

Then the chorus of cheers and battle cries rang out. The words were not of Levanthrian tongue.

"Well," Vorax said, "Morvin wanted a distraction."

"I don't think this was what he had in mind," Darmour answered as they looked at one another with concern. Vorax lowered a murmuring Zerina as she stirred from unconsciousness.

"What happened?" she groaned, unsteady on her feet.

"We are under attack from the Zarubians," Vorax answered as she removed her axe from her back.

"Go, fight," said Zerina. "I will be okay. I just need to gather my bearings."

"I won't leave you," Darmour protested.

Zerina gazed into Darmour's eyes. "Morvin and Skyrar are going to need all the help they can get now," she said. "You must get to the keep!"

"What about you?"

"I will remain here. My magic is powerful enough to help on the front line."

Darmour removed his cutlass. "Come with us," he begged.

"These soldiers need me."

The determined look in her eyes was all too familiar, and Darmour knew that nothing he could say would change her mind.

"As soon as you get an opportunity, you head to the keep," he said.

He gave her one last, lingering look, hoping she already knew all the things that were left unsaid in that moment.

With that, Darmour and Vorax set off in the direction of the keep, leaving Zerina behind.

Out of the darkness, the roars grew louder and louder until the clattering of steel against steel rang out in the night, and screams of pain and anger erupted as the two armies clashed. It was chaos as Levanthrian soldiers attempted to mobilise from a state of disarray. Storm and flame magic fired out as flashes of yellow, orange, and blue lit up the sky.

Zarubians shot out from between the tents with their twin bladed weapons and flooded into the camp. Their warriors were thin and wiry, their hair tied back as they darted through the shadows. The speed with which they moved surprised Darmour as he witnessed one of them slice through three soldiers with shocking precision.

The Zarubians were headed straight for him and Vorax.

"Suicide warriors," Vorax said. "Fast and efficient, they see death on the battlefield as an honour granted by the gods. They are the first line of attack." She brought up her axe in front of her. "The worst thing you can do is wait for them to reach you. May the gods watch over you, Darmour." With this, Vorax launched herself forward to the attacking Zarubians. There were two in front of her, both carrying twin blades.

Vorax roared as she turned into a spin, gaining as much momentum as she could with alarming speed for her size. When her axe met the middle of one of the Zarubians, she met him with such force, such velocity, that she cleaved the man in two before continuing her spin. As she brought herself to a stop, her axe met the chest of the other Zarubian, who found their chest exploding from the impact before her axe drove them to the floor. As a third attacker approached, she rammed the pole of the axe into their face, then lunged forward with an almighty boot to the chest. Her axe was already raised before the warrior hit the ground, and she brought it down on top of him with a sickening crunch.

Darmour found himself in awe of her brutality, her speed ten times more impressive given her size.

He snapped away as the cry of a nearby Zarubian caught his attention. He turned to see the soldier already upon him, their two swords swinging sideways towards him. He barely ducked the strike, his chest thundering as he turned to face his attacker. Like the other Zarubians, this one was slender and athletic in build, clad in lightweight, dark-red leather.

He brought his swords down on Darmour who raised his blade sideways to block the strike. As steel met steel, the Zarubian pressed down against Darmour as he struggled with his weaker arm. He could still fight with a blade; he had often practiced with his weaker hand all throughout his life – something his father had always drummed into him when he was younger. He had resented his father's strict and relentless training regimen at the time, but in this moment, it was something he was grateful for.

Both warriors grimaced and growled until Darmour pushed the Zarubian soldier back before striking out. They exchanged blows over and over, the sound of steel chiming in the air amongst the screams and the roars.

Flames had begun to spread from tent to tent. The harshness of the heat stung Darmour's face as he looked for an opening in his opponent's defences. Another blast of magic landed beside them, spraying them with sand. The force knocked them both over, and it took a few moments for Darmour to gather himself, his ears ringing with a high-pitched noise that caused his eyes to sting and blur. As the noise subsided, the Zarubian wasted no time diving on top of Darmour with one of his blades. Darmour reached up and grabbed hold of the warrior's wrist, holding him in place. He brought up his weakened arm and smashed it into the side of the Zarubian's head. The flash of pain was agonising as his stump made contact. It was a nauseating pain, but one he knew he needed to endure if he was going to survive.

It was enough to throw the warrior off balance, and Darmour used his weight to roll the man off him. Wasting no time, he pummelled him with his fist over and over again.

When the soldier's arms slumped from unconsciousness, Darmour reached for the nearest blade and grabbed hold of it before bringing it down into his stomach. The Zarubian let out a gargled noise as air bubbled in the blood that filled his mouth.

Panting heavily, Darmour brought himself to his feet. Around him, the battle had engulfed the camp. Levanthrian forces battled fiercely against the Zarubians, and bodies lay slain in the sand, the flames whipping up a fierce heat.

Darmour sought to reach Vorax who fought farther

ahead. He quickly dispatched another three Zarubians who got in his way, slicing his cutlass through their stomachs and across their chests. Their choice in armour may have been helping them with their speed, but it was making it easier to lay them to waste in open combat.

Darmour watched as Vorax brought down her axe onto a soldier she had knocked to the ground, their blood splashing into the air as though Vorax had jumped into a puddle with glee.

"Vorax!" Darmour called. She turned towards him, her face covered in the red of her enemies. There was a snarl there that Darmour had not seen before. Battle rage had definitely taken her.

Another Zarubian ran from the shadows, swords outstretched and poised to strike the Elven warrior. Darmour rushed forward, driving his blade into the back of the attacker just in time.

"It's a fine day for a battle," Darmour shouted over the chaos.

Vorax's breathing was heavy as she panted, allowing herself a moment to gather herself from her blood lust. "We need to reach the keep," she said, racing off towards the castle. Her axe swung every time someone got close to her.

"Fall back!" Captain Xerij's voice bellowed from beyond the darkness. "We need to protect the keep, we need to protect the king!"

The command would make it that much harder for Darmour and Vorax to aid Morvin and Skyrar, but first they needed to survive the attack.

Darmour desperately hoped that Zerina was all right. Magical blasts littered the sky and their surroundings, rendering it impossible for him to ascertain which magic was hers.

"This way," Vorax said as she pushed towards the front of the keep through the jostling crowd of retreating soldiers. Blasts of magic continued to pepper the dirt around them, each blast sending shock waves rippling through the ground as wood and stone sprayed into them, grazing and cutting their skin as they ran. When they reached the open ground just in front of the keep, Darmour saw the stocks where they had been held for three days, and beside them, the gate to the keep was closed.

Another wave of Levanthrian soldiers were sprinting towards them, ashen faced and panic-stricken as they made for the keep.

"It's a fucking massacre," Captain Xerij said, joining Darmour and Vorax. "We need to defend this spot with the soldiers that we have left. Mages, buy us some time!"

Some mages stepped forward and began channelling their powers, their faces grimacing with pain as they cast the barrier spells. They did their best at repelling the magical blasts that were raining down on them, but some Zarubian flames still managed to force their way through. One soldier screamed a final scream as a blast of fire landed straight on top of him, his body evaporating in an instant as the magical flames engulfed him.

Darmour frantically searched the crowd, but there was still no sign of Zerina.

Captain Xerij ran in front of the mages. There were still plenty of Levanthrian soldiers in front of the keep, too many for Darmour to count.

"Get in formation!" Captain Xerij bellowed. "I'd be damned if we were to fail on this day!" The soldiers seemed to take spirit in Captain Xerij's presence. As instructed, they began to quickly form multiple lines of defence.

"Pikemen at the front, mages behind, the rest of you with me." Captain Xerij raised her sword into the air.

Darmour eyed up the entranceway to the keep. There was no way to get inside and nowhere to run. To turn their backs on such an enemy would be foolish at best and cowardice at worst.

"We making this stand?" Darmour asked Vorax who looked down on him fiercely, the hilt of her battle axe gripped tightly in her hand.

"I don't see any other way," she said. "As soon as the opportunity arises to get into the keep, we take it."

Darmour and Vorax moved to take up position with the other soldiers.

"Where the fuck is Reve?" Xerij spat as she stared into the flaming camp in front of them.

"Maybe he has fallen," Darmour said.

"I guarantee the fucking coward ran at the first sign of the battle," she scoffed. "These soldiers need leaders, not cowards."

The magical blasts stopped as suddenly as they had started. The crackling of the burning camp was louder than the screams of those taking their final breaths. Swords clashed as Levanthrian soldiers bravely took their last stand against the Zarubian forces.

Then an eerie silence took aver.

Darmour stared into the lit-up sky and the darkness that surrounded the camp. A wave of anxious anticipation filled the air that felt as charged as storm magic.

"Hold steady!" Captain Xerij's cracked, dry voice broke the silence as the soldiers maintained position. At the front of the line, the pikemen raised their weapons. Around a dozen mages stood behind them, with the rest of the Levanthrians stood in multiple rows behind them. As

Darmour looked down the line of soldiers beside him, he found it ironic that after so many years sailing the high seas as a pirate, his final moments would be spent fighting as a soldier in the Levanthrian army.

The king's army.

The faces of every man and woman who stood beside him were decorated with varying looks of worry, fear, bravery, and determination.

Ahead of them through the shadows and the flames, the Zarubian forces slowly stepped into sight. These ones were better equipped for battle, unlike the leatherbound soldiers that Darmour had been fighting against.

They wore steel armour, plates, and chainmail, with the red of Zarubia on their banners and tunics. Their armour was sleek and well fitted, finely crafted by their blacksmiths.

"Hold your defences," Captain Xerij commanded. "Let's show these Zarubians what we are capable of. For the king, and for Levanthria!"

A chorus of cheers boomed from the soldiers as they readied themselves to make a stand.

And Darmour realised he would die defending the very king they had come here to kill.

23

The ground rumbled as if an earthquake had hit.

Morvin and Skyrar's immediate surroundings lit up in a flash as a large plume of smoke filled the sky on the far side of the camp.

"Shit!" Skyrar said. "Was that your powder?"

"I think so?" Morvin said as he studied the chasm of smoke rising from the blast. His eyes lit up with wonder and concern at the size of the blast. Even he hadn't estimated it being that powerful.

"That didn't take them long," Skyrar said, an impressed look on her face.

"I hope they are okay," Morvin mused, lifting his remaining barrel of powder. "Come on, we don't have long."

The two of them left the tent to see if the pathway towards the northern point of the keep was clear. A patrol of soldiers quickly ran past them, their weapons drawn.

"There is only so long an Elven warrior and a crippled pirate can fight for," Skyrar said.

"Then we best not let the distraction they have caused

go to waste," Morvin said pensively. Something didn't look right as more blasts rained down on the camp, fire balls erupting at scattered points.

"What's wrong?" Skyrar asked.

"I didn't think the powder would do that. Something seems off," Morvin said as another patrol ran past them down the path and towards the explosions. Cries started reaching them, sword against sword chiming in the air like a nightmarish lullaby.

"It's the Zarubians!" Morvin heard one soldier shout as they ran past.

"Zarubians?" Morvin muttered. "As if tonight was not already difficult enough."

They set off down the darkened path, the sky behind them illuminated with flashes of fire and storm magic which lit up the path ahead. Flames ripped through camp as men and women started screaming out in pain as they were tortured by the magic.

"Keep going," Morvin demanded as he thundered down the path with Skyrar beside him. The barrel was heavy, but it was the shape of the barrel that made it difficult to carry, with the bottom digging into Morvin's fingers.

"What about the others?" Skyrar asked. "They are not merely creating a distraction, they are fighting a battle."

"They know what they must do, as do we. There is a high chance that we do not make it back from this. It's something I have made peace with, lass. I suggest you do the same."

With the patrolling soldiers heading into camp to fight, the path remained clear, meaning they could traverse the back of the keep as they searched for the drains that General Precian had told Morvin about.

"Just my luck to be left with a fucking Dwarf on a

suicide mission." Skyrar looked down at Morvin in frustration. "No offence."

"None taken." Morvin smiled and was surprised to see Skyrar do the same.

"Guess we best get in this keep," Skyrar hissed, looking up at the fort as they climbed a small embankment. If not for the battle on the other side of camp, their approach would have been much harder with them needing to evade the watch of patrols inside. Either way, the battle had served to provide the very distraction that they had desired. Their feet sank into the sand as they continued their ascent to the base of the keep, Morvin's legs burning as his breath heaved, a little rasp escaping his lungs.

"Where are these drains?" Skyrar asked as they followed the curvature of the wall. The stone was almost white, far lighter than the darker stone used within Levanthria.

Morvin pointed. "Over there." A hole surrounded by green moss sat in the stone, the green growth climbing down the side of the keep as if it sought to escape itself. Below it sat a trench dug out in the sand where bodily fluids had met it, carving its way down the embankment. When they reached it, Morvin looked inside, but he couldn't see anything, only darkness. The stench of piss and shit greeted him like an unwanted handshake, and he turned his head as he nearly gagged.

"Fuck!" Skyrar said, her voice elevated. "This is not how I envisioned the plan when Tarin recruited me."

"We need to do this for Tarin, so that his efforts were not in vain." Morvin paused and took another look inside the drain. It was going to be snug for him, let alone the barrel with his thick shoulders and Dwarven frame. Less so for Skyrar. "Ladies first?" Morvin gestured.

"Fuck off!" she spat. "This is your plan. You can lead the

way. Just don't slip and slide into me! Now, can we get this next part over and done with?"

Morvin took a deep breath away from the opening. The air itself tasted tainted as the stench kissed the back of his nose and throat. Even his posting shovelling shit had not prepared him to wade through it on his arms and belly. He psyched himself up before standing in front of the opening, giving it one last look.

"See you on the other side," he said. He pushed the barrel inside before he reached in arms first and started to crawl up the narrow space using his elbows, shoving the barrel upwards as he moved. There was enough waste to ensure that the stone remained uncomfortably damp as Morvin continued to crawl, yet he pushed through the waves of nausea as he pressed forward, his arms aching deeply as he struggled beneath the weight of the powder. His shoulders pressed against the stone on either side of him, taking more of an effort to squeeze himself through the space as he sat on a constant edge of gagging.

"I can't believe we are doing this," Skyrar spoke though congested breath from behind him.

"Shhh," Morvin replied. "Our voices could travel up the drain. Only the gods know what is waiting for us up there." He continued to dig deep as he slowly forced his way up through the drain, keeping focused on why he was stooping to such depths.

He would avenge his wife and son.

The drain widened and narrowed at different parts as they continued through the dark. With nothing but the stench to guide them, Morvin used his anger, his hatred for the king, to fuel the fire that burned deep within him, like the white-hot embers of a forge. In this darkened place, the battle that was raging outside was muffled by the stone that surrounded them. Aside from the odd rumble that they felt through the stone, they might have forgotten that there was a battle raging outside.

Something ahead caught Morvin's attention and the flicker of a flame ahead of him caused his mood to lift. "Not long now, lass," he whispered as he continued to drag himself upwards, his elbows now stinging and raw from the jagged stone underneath him. When he reached the top, he poked his head from the hole that was carved through the stone and took in a huge gulp of air. It wasn't pure but it felt crisper than Garuvian ice as he savoured it.

Luckily no one else was around in the toilet, and Morvin sought to pull himself free. "Coast is clear," he said.

"Then hurry up," Skyrar's muffled voice harried him, and Morvin felt a shove on his backside as he was forced up out of the toilet. He gathered himself, then went back to the opening to help pull Skyrar free.

The door to the room swung open.

Morvin instinctively jumped behind the door as one soldier entered and the door closed behind him. He undid his trousers and stood over the hole where Skyrar lay hidden. He sighed as he readied himself to relieve his bladder. When he looked down, his face was awash with shock at the hazel eyes and pale face that greeted him.

"What the —"

In a flash, Skyrar sliced upwards with a dagger, dismembering the soldier as he squealed like a pig. Morvin shot from behind him and jumped up onto his back, covering his mouth as the soldier started to buck, his blood spraying around the room from his groin.

Morvin held on tightly, not wanting to draw further attention to them through the screams of the guard. With a display of agility, Skyrar shot from the toilet and pressed her dagger slowly through the guard's chin with a crunch. The soldier stopped bucking and fell to the floor with Morvin jumping back from him just in time.

"Was there any need?" Morvin asked, eyes wide at the appendage which lay on the stone floor.

"It was either that or be pissed on," Skyrar said coldly, "and no quest is worth that."

"Although I hear some would gladly pay for a service like that," Morvin laughed, then quietened himself, remembering where they were.

Skyrar curled her face up in disgust. "Animals," she said before reaching for the door and opening it slowly. "There are three soldiers ahead. Likely they will be waiting for this one to return. Which way do we need to go?"

"Where's Dravo?" one of soldiers said impatiently. "We need to get to the king's chambers. We are under attack!"

Morvin racked his brain. "I don't know," he admitted. "The general merely said that the powder needed to go to the cellar below the king's chambers."

Skyrar rolled her eyes in disbelief before eyeing up the group of soldiers ahead of them. "Leave these to me." She slid into the shadows against the wall, vanishing out of Morvin's sight. He crept to the door to look on.

From the shadows beside the group, she shot out with her blade, slicing the neck of one soldier before pushing another against the wall and slamming her dagger into his chest with brutal efficiency. Before the third guard had time to react, she had already pulled a second dagger from her waist and rammed it into her stomach. She pulled her other dagger free and brought it around, piling it into the side of the soldier's mouth. The speed with which she moved shocked Morvin. Had he blinked, he would not have seen her in action.

The three soldiers dropped in unison to the floor, their lives ruthlessly ended in the blink of an eye.

Skyrar looked farther down the corridor before waving Morvin over. He gave another look down the adjacent corridor before following her.

"This place is bigger than it looks from the outside," she said as Morvin approached, wiping the blood off her daggers on her arms.

"Keep to the inner edge and follow the wall. We will likely find a staircase. Let's hope we don't bump into any more soldiers, and that they don't find these bodies," he said.

Skyrar smirked. "I hope they do."

The two of them followed the inside wall until they reached a staircase. Luckily, they did not find any other soldiers, and the opening to the stairs was illuminated by a torch on either side. Morvin grabbed one of them and took the steps down into the basement.

His chest pounded as they reached another chamber that was lined with doors. When Morvin tried the first, he found that it was locked.

"Skyrar, if you would."

Skyrar removed a pick from her pockets and inserted it into the lock. After a brief moment, there was a click from inside and she pushed the door open. There was nothing inside.

"Who locks a fucking door to nothing?" she scoffed as she moved on to the next door. It did not take long for her to unlock it and she kicked it open. The room was lined with oak barrels, similar to the ones they had fetched the powder in.

"I think the king's room is above the room behind that door, can you pick it?"

Skyrar scowled at Morvin and set to work on the lock as Morvin rolled the barrel just behind her.

"As soon as you open the door, I'll place the barrel in the centre of the room."

Skyrar continued to concentrate on the lock as she attempted to pick it, cursing under her breath.

"Hurry, lass, we have no time to spare," he said, eyeing up the door.

"I'm trying. This lock is different from the others." She wriggled the pick in her hands whilst listening to the door before the familiar click noise came from within. With a smug smile, Skyrar pulled the door back. Morvin poked his head in to find two barrels side by side and he joined Skyrar with smiling.

"This is it," he said. "It's the moment we have been waiting for. I only hope the king remains in his chambers above." Morvin stepped forward to carry the powder into the cellar. They were so close now, all they needed to do was ignite it.

"What do you mean by that?" came a voice from behind them.

Morvin's blood ran cold as he turned to see Captain Reve in the doorway. He had a crossbow aimed directly at them.

Before either of them had time to move, he pulled the trigger and fired an arrow into Skyrar's torso. She stumbled backwards into the room as Captain Reve turned to aim the crossbow straight at Morvin's face.

24

"Hold your nerves," Captain Xerij demanded as the Zarubian forces advanced towards them. Darmour could see that their numbers far exceeded their own.

"We do not break formation," she added as wavering arms of the first line of defence held their pikes aloft.

The Zarubians advanced for a short distance before stopping, the two forces eyeing up one another. Flames danced behind them as their soldiers took up their offensive formation. Their commander stepped to the front of their lines and raised his helmet. His armour was larger than the others. He was clearly of high rank, a knight perhaps.

"Lay down your weapons and submit," he said aggressively. "You have invaded our lands and slaughtered our people. I offer you a kindness compared to what your king has shown us. All I ask is for your king's head on a spike!"

"For the king!" Captain Xerij called back.

The rest of the shoulders repeating her words in unison.

"FOR THE KING!"

All except for Darmour and Vorax, who remained silent as they stared down at their enemy.

"Very well," the commander said with a smile. "I prefer it this way." He lowered the visor of his helmet which reflected the flames that lit up the dark sky. With a wave of his arms, his soldiers advanced forward, some on foot, some on horseback.

"Hold," Captain Xerij called as she stepped into a defensive stance, holding her sword behind her, ready to strike.

As the wave of Zarubian soldiers met the Levanthrian forces, battle cries rang out once more as the pikemen held firm. Bodies found themselves impaled, as with horses. There were groans of agony and screams of death from both sides.

"Mages!" Captain Xerij threw her sword forward and the mages returned fire with varying spells, blasting into the chests of the advancing soldiers. The Zarubians formed a red sea of dark-red armour. Soon they had engulfed the mages as they pushed through the pikemen, swallowing them with their superior force. The Zarubians seemed happy to sacrifice some of their soldiers to drown the Levanthrian forces in their numbers.

Xerij let out an almighty roar as she brought her sword up against the first Zarubian that reached her. Within seconds, the two forces had blended into one.

Within the mass of bodies was chaos. Darmour began hacking and slashing at any Zarubian that came near him. It was like slicing through vines as he took them down. Vorax roared her own battle cry as she cleaved the head off an advancing soldier before barging into the side of a horse whose rider was bringing their sword down on Levanthrian soldiers. The horse toppled over, its rider's leg trapped underneath. Vorax vaulted the horse, landing on the other side. She brought her blood-soaked axe above her head with a growl before slamming it down on the fallen rider.

Captain Xerij, displaying her battle prowess, exchanged strikes with many as she danced her way through the battle, leaving nothing but a trail of bodies behind her. Out of the corner of his eye, Darmour saw her enter the path of the enemy commander. The two stopped for a moment, eyeing each other up. Then Xerij lunged forward with her sword raised, but the Zarubian knight parried her strike with ease, swinging his own sword to meet hers. The blow forced her backwards. She just about managed to keep her footing, but the knight was already upon her. He brought down his sword once again, then again. Xerij continued to parry the strikes, struggling with the knight's strength and speed which was unhindered even by the thick armour he wore.

Levanthrian soldiers were dropping fast as the Zarubians swarmed their forces. Darmour looked around him as they continued to fight in vain.

"You want the king's head?" he roared as he ducked the strike of an advancing soldier. "I will bring it to you myself!" He brought his cutlass down onto the skull of the Zarubian warrior, then glanced back at the keep, its locked metal gate keeping them out.

Somehow, they needed to get inside.

"Vorax!" Darmour roared. "Vorax!" Scores of Zarubians crashed into the ground as she smashed through them like a battering ram, her armour soaked in the blood of her enemies.

"There's too many!" she cried.

"We can end this battle. We just need to get inside!"

In the middle of the battle, a weary Xerij continued to fight against the knight, slashing at him and blocking his attacks against her. Her arms appeared to be growing tired as her sword became heavier and heavier with every strike that she threw. The knight continued to push against Xerij who was only just able to cling on to her sword, each strike taking her longer and longer to recover from.

There was nothing they could do for the captain now. Darmour and Vorax began to fall back towards the gates at the entranceway to the keep.

Then the earth began to shake beneath their feet. Darmour and Vorax stopped in their tracks and turned around to see what the source of the quake was.

The Zarubian knight had taken a step back, and pulsating energy was emanating from within him. He pushed his free hand forward and sent another unseen blast of magic into the ground. The rumbling of the earth intensified as pits of sand opened up around the knight and Xerij, swallowing up any soldier who was unfortunate enough to fall into its path.

Xerij only just managed to keep her balance, her feet sinking into the sand as the ground continued to shake with vigorous force.

Darmour looked on in shock as men and women from both sides fell into pits that had formed in the sand. He had no idea how deep they were, or if any soldiers falling in would survive.

His question was answered when the sand started falling in on itself from the vibrations of the quake, pouring in on top of the poor souls below.

Beyond the chaos, Xerij continued to fight against the knight, even with her feet sinking further and further into the ground.

"We need to help!" Darmour said. "There won't be any soldiers left if we do not take down their battle mage."

The knight raised a clenched fist into the air and slammed it into the ground, causing another quake.

"A battle mage?" Vorax said. "Sounds like a great way to test my steel." She clicked her neck as if savouring the challenge.

Against their better judgement, the two of them raced through the battlefield to aid the captain in her fight against the Zarubian commander. The battle between the two forces continued fiercely. Levanthrian soldiers continued fighting bravely despite being greatly outnumbered. In front of the keep, the main line of defence remained in formation as the ranks in front of them took the fight to the Zarubians.

Darmour ran as fast as he could, the sand making it difficult terrain to navigate at speed. They covered the ground quickly and soon found themselves nearing the captain as she took an almighty swing of her sword, gripping the hilt with both hands. The knight knocked her blade from her hands and Captain Xerij looked up unapologetically at the knight before roaring and pulling a dagger from her side.

The knight slammed his sword into the ground and grabbed hold of her wrist as she lunged for him. With his free hand, he clasped it tightly against the side of her head.

"No!" Darmour roared as he dug as deep as he could to get to her as fast as possible.

He was not quick enough.

The knight channelled his powers down his arm and forced his quake magic into Captain Xerij's head. She screamed out in pain as blood streamed from her eyes, then began pouring from her nose, ears, and mouth. With a blast of magic, her head exploded, sending bone and brain splattering into the sand. Darmour and Vorax were not quick enough to help the captain, but Darmour would be damned if he let anyone else suffer her fate.

Darmour swung his cutlass down as soon as he reached the knight. The Zarubian commander stepped back, searching behind him for his sword, which remained embedded in the sand. Not wanting to lose momentum, Darmour kept swinging, each time the knight ducking and dodging the strikes.

Reaching behind him, the battle mage grabbed the hilt of his blade and swung it towards Darmour.

The pirate raised his sword to parry away the strike. The strain on his arm was immense, and he turned into the blade, pressing his forearm against the back of his other to reinforce the block.

Vorax shot past Darmour and leapt into the air with her axe high above her, garnering the knight's attention. He stepped to the side as Vorax's axe cut through the air. He turned, bringing his sword down on her. Darmour instinctively dived into the knight shoulder first. Slamming into the metal armour sent pain coursing down his left side, but it was enough to throw the knight off balance. His blade cut down the side of Vorax's arm instead of delivering a killing blow.

The Zarubian let out a roar of frustration and slammed his fist into the ground again, sending out a rippling shock wave that sent everyone in the vicinity crashing to the ground.

The knight stood over Vorax and attempted to skewer her into the ground where she lay collapsed in a heap.

But he was knocked off his balance once more, this time by a blast of fire magic that crashed into his armour.

With a roar, he grabbed hold of his red-hot shoulder pauldron and ripped it from him, tossing it to the ground. As he looked for the source of the blast, his attention removed from Vorax and Darmour who used the brief reprieve to get back to their feet.

Zerina shot through the crowd of warring soldiers, her gaze fixed on the knight as she weaved in and out of the soldiers between them. One of her arms was lit up in molten flame as she used her hand like a blade against any Zarubian who got in her way, her strikes slicing through their armour like a knife through butter. She rolled her shoulder back and fired another blast of fire at the knight who took the full force in his other shoulder, the pauldron burning red. He dropped his sword and scrambled to remove the metal armour as it seared into his skin.

Sensing an opportunity, Darmour leapt up and buried his cutlass into the knight's now-exposed shoulder, tearing through his flesh. It felt as though he were embedding his weapon in stone.

Against a normal man, the strike would have easily detached his arm from his shoulder, but this was not a normal man. The knight slammed his metal fist into the side of Damour's head. He saw a flash of light as he crashed into the ground. The knight grabbed hold of the cutlass and pulled it from his shoulder with a growl of pain, then tossed it onto the ground.

The Zarubian commander readied himself to slam his boot down onto a dazed Darmour's head, only to have to adjust as Vorax roared and threw a punch at him. He grabbed hold of her fist, the two of them of equal height. Then Vorax brought down her free fist onto his injury.

This seemed to only anger him more. He squeezed down on Vorax's hand which started to crack and crunch under the pressure. Vorax grimaced as the knight focused his magic once more. Still dazed from the blow, Darmour struggled to get back to his feet as he watched Vorax trying in vain to release her hand from the Zarubian's grasp.

The knight was too strong, too powerful.

Vorax used her free hand to rip his helmet from his face, revealing the angered face of the battle mage underneath. His dark eyes burned into her with an unforgiving gaze as she used her weight to roll her body behind him, pulling his arm across his chest as she grappled him from behind.

"End him!" she said, trembling as she held him in place.

Zerina stopped in front of them, her arm still glowing white-hot. "Get out of the way, Vorax!"

"Just do it!"

The knight continued to struggle against Vorax's strength. He closed his eyes and started to concentrate his quake magic once more, and his energy visibly pulsated through him and into Vorax. A trail of blood began to trail from Vorax's nostril, her eyes becoming bloodshot.

"Now!" Vorax roared. "It's the only way!"

Zerina forced her hand back and fired a focused blast of fire into the night. A stream of fire engulfed the battle mage in his entirety as Vorax attempted to shield herself.

Zerina's expression was that of agony as her magic ripped through her body, the blast of magic maintaining a fierce well of fire.

Darmour pushed himself to his feet, fighting off a wave of nausea.

When it seemed that Vorax couldn't hold on any longer, she collapsed on the ground, the armour on her arms melting, her flesh burnt beyond repair.

Zerina stopped her magic and the Zarubian knight staggered backwards, his armour molten as he screamed in agony. It was at this moment that Darmour stepped in front of him with the knight's own sword and jammed it into the exposed burnt flesh of his chest. The sword went through him in its entirety. The knight's eyes grew wide before he exhaled his last breath and slumped back into the sand.

"Vorax!" Darmour called, dropping to her side as he inspected her wounds. She wheezed heavily with each agonising breath, a whistle leaving her chest. "That was fucking stupid!" he scolded. Her hair was singed back to her scalp, leaving crisp red and black skin all down one side of her face.

"I did – what needed – to be done," she managed to muster the words through cracked, pained breath.

"Zerina, do something," Darmour demanded as Zerina raised her hands and placed them against the hot metal on Vorax's arm.

"My axe," Vorax said. "I am beyond repair. Pass me my axe." She laughed, and blood left her mouth, covering her chin.

"Her wounds are too grave," Zerina said. She closed her eyes as tears fell down her pale cheeks.

Darmour passed Vorax her axe, guiding her trembling hands around its handle. Clutching the weapon to her chest, Vorax rested her head back into the sand. In this moment, it was as if there was only the three of them there in the midst of the battle.

"Help the others," Vorax gasped. "I take solitude in knowing that in my death, I will soon greet the king in the afterlife." Her eyes remained wide as a rasping croak left her lungs and she took her final breaths.

"I am so sorry," Zerina said, her cheeks sodden with tears.

"She was a brave warrior," Darmour said, bowing his head. "The bravest."

"Look!" Zerina suddenly pointed out towards the camp.

They both stood in dread at the sight before them.

More Zarubians had entered the battlefield. A wall of red soldiers that would surely wipe them all out.

25

"Answer my question, Dwarf," Captain Reve sneered, his crossbow firmly pointed at Morvin.

Skyrar sat stooped again the wall, her hands wrapped around the arrow that protruded from her abdomen. Blood pooled around her.

"I think you know the answer to that," Morvin said, raising his hands to either side of his head. "The question, is Captain, what are *you* doing in here, when there is a battle out there?"

Captain Reve looked flustered at Morvin's question. "I think you will find it is me with the bow." He shook the crossbow in his direction. "I knew you and the others could not be trusted when you arrived in camp. Just think what riches the king will give me when he learns that I foiled a plot to assassinate him."

"I will do what I need to, Captain," Morvin warned.

"Just what is it you are planning on doing from here?" Reve leant to his right to peer into the open chamber where Skyrar sat bleeding out. "Just what is it that you have in there?"

"A means to an end." Morvin's reply was short and sharp. He had no time for fools. "We have come too far to fall at this stage," he said dryly. "I will not allow myself to be stopped by a coward like you. You hide in the keep while your men fight."

"I don't think you are exactly in a position to lecture me about cowardice. GAURDS!" Reve bellowed, his voice echoing up the stairs.

Morvin lunged forward and grabbed hold of the crossbow, forcing it upwards just as a bolt fired from it and ricocheted off the stone ceiling. He grappled with Reve, managing to knock the crossbow to the floor. He had dreamed of this moment for so long, and Morvin clenched his fist tightly before ramming it into Reve's midriff, forcing an oafish puff of air from him.

Reve threw a punch at Morvin but it was clear that this man was no fighter. Morvin, already standing a good two feet shorter, ducked under the blow before jabbing into Reve's torso once more. Then he planted a full boot into Reve's backside and sent him straight into the room where the powder sat. As he stumbled through the doorway, Skyrar stretched out a leg, causing Reve to trip over and crash into the barrel. The barrel toppled from the force, the lid popping off and the powder pouring over the floor.

Morvin grabbed Reve by the scruff of his neck and pummelled his face, his hatred for him on full display.

"You can't do this! It's – it's treason!"

"It's no more than the king deserves, for all the suffering he has inflicted on these lands, on his own people." Morvin slammed his fist into Reve's face once more before letting go of him as he slumped on the ground in a daze.

"You okay, lass?" He turned to see Skyrar struggling on the ground, her blood spreading in a wide circle around her.

"What do you think?" she spoke through gritted teeth and tried to pull herself up, but she was too weak. "Mix the powder," she told him. "You need to move quickly before more soldiers arrive."

Morvin set about using a shovel to quickly mix the powder together even more, the glow becoming brighter and brighter as it became ready to ignite.

Steps on stone alerted Morvin to approaching guards. Skyrar was closest to the doorway. She reached for a dagger and launched it at the stairwell just as a soldier appeared. He ran straight into the blade as it buried deep into his chest. More soldiers approached as Morvin shot into the doorway to buy them time.

"Here." Morvin reached into his tunic and produced the small flint device. He eyed it briefly before tossing it to Skyrar. "Make yourself useful." The flint device landed on her legs as Morvin removed Herelda from his back. The weapon he had spent years creating, honing, so that when it needed to be called upon, it would be ready.

He had already fired it once against the scorpion, and he did not know if it would shoot a second time. But Morvin had spent so long tinkering with it, adapting its design to make it as deadly as he could. It was already loaded with powder, and he aimed it at the approaching soldiers.

He was about to find out if his tinkering had worked.

Morvin brought his hand down on the side of the chamber and rolled it. With a click, the cylinder turned, and Morvin pulled the trigger again.

With a flash of light, the powerful blast forced itself from the end of Herelda, piercing through the first soldier's chest, then the second and the third soldier behind him. All three were blasted backwards with the force of a trebuchet. Their chests had been cleaved open, leaving nothing but mashed up organs and bones on display.

"Go!" Skyrar demanded. "Get to the king! You need to make sure he does not leave that chamber, and if he does, you end him!"

"Give me that," Reve growled as he dived at Skyrar, grabbing hold of her wrist.

"Go!" she shouted as she pulled out her remaining dagger and jammed it into the side of Reve's torso.

Reve staggered backwards, looking shocked. "You – you stabbed me, " he spluttered, clasping his hands over his wound.

"And you shot me. Not that that makes us even. You can join me in the afterlife." She turned and nodded to Morvin. "Go!" she hissed weakly.

Morvin hurtled towards the stairs. He needed to get to the upper level, to find the king's chamber to ensure that he did not make it out alive.

Between the battle raging outside and the guards they had killed whose bodies would undoubtedly be discovered, all he had time for now was a direct confrontation with the king.

When he reached the top of the stairs, daylight had begun to shine through the windows. Ahead of him, a guard rushed towards him, and Morvin dropped down onto one knee, pointing Herelda at the advancing guard. With a boom, another blast of metal and magic propelled out and straight into the man without the need for reloading. The guard spattered against the wall, his torso nothing but a bloody pulp.

As Morvin reached the next flight of steps, the ground

shook as if they were in an earthquake. A blast of light over-took Morvin and stone exploded behind him.

Skyrar had succeeded in igniting the powder.

The blast sent Morvin crashing into the stone steps as he desperately tried to climb them to the next floor. Soot and dust filled every pocket of air as the stone above crumbled and shook, the noise of the blast causing Morvin's ears to ring. The plume of dust made it impossible for Morvin to see. He staggered to the top of the stairs, the keep crumbling around him.

He struggled to breathe as dust and smoke filled his chest and he heaved his body onto the next floor. The air was clearer here, but the keep continued to rumble from the explosion. His powder had worked exactly as intended; the blast had been tremendous, far more powerful than Morvin had even anticipated. Stone continued to rumble around him as cracks formed in the stone underfoot and up the walls. Morvin continued to follow the corridor around until flames from the battleground could be seen in the distance. He brought himself to a stop as he looked out over the fighting.

Where walls once stood, nothing but crumbling ruins now lay. The blast from the powder had blown a hole in the entire southern side of the keep.

There was no sign of life, and the stone behind him fell in on itself like a maelstrom in the ocean as if some unseen force was pulling what remained of the keep in on itself. The floor beneath him shook again and Morvin lost his footing, tumbling towards the edge. The fire from the battlefield spun around him as he dropped down onto the crumbled stone below. With another blast, the stone above him continued to fall as his body landed in a crumpled heap on the jagged stone ruins.

26

"How are we meant to fight off all of these?" Darmour said. "And where the fuck is Ulrik!" Darmour gripped his cutlass tightly as he stared out at the open field of the advancing Zarubian army.

"I will do what I can," Zerina said, her face glowing from her ignited arm.

Darmour gave her a smile. "With you by my side, I would fight any army." He would be damned if he did not let Zerina know how he felt if this was to be their final moment. He wrapped his arms around her and pulled her towards him. In a flash, her arm stopped glowing with flames, and she brought her hand up and placed it tenderly on his chest.

The two of them shared a kiss amongst a mass of warring soldiers.

When Darmour pulled away, he took a moment to stare into her blue eyes. "When all this is done, promise me you will find that spark inside your heart again. You can't only live for Ulrik."

"I made a promise to him, to keep his sister safe. That is what I must do, Darmour. You know this. I will do what I must to keep those whom I care about safe." With this, Zerina turned to face the battlefield and channelled her magic through her arm once more, the molten flames tracing down her skin. Flickers of fire danced from her skin with a magical glow. "Help me get to the front," she said. "I will do what I can."

"Aye," Darmour said, and the two of them pushed through the ensuing battle, Darmour striking down anyone that got in their way. Zerina fired blast after blast of magic as the Zarubians rained down their own fire and storm magic onto the battlefield. Bodies flew through the air as the magic bounced around them. The chaos was unspeakable, like nothing Darmour had ever witnessed. When they reached the opposite side of the Zarubian reinforcements, Zerina and Darmour were all that stood in the way of their army's victory.

"Buy me some time," Zerina said. She then began chanting an incantation that Darmour had not heard before.

As two Zarubians approached, Darmour began trading blows with them, parrying away attacks as they tried to cleave him in half with their weapons. Fighting was so much harder with one hand, yet it did not deter Darmour. With Zerina by his side, he had everything of value next to him and he would not let any harm come to her.

Darmour rushed forward and drove his blade through the stomach of one Zarubian before using his free arm to grapple the body. He spun as the other soldier bought down his axe, embedding it into the back of the soldier Darmour had just killed. He pushed the body forward to give him some space. The remaining Zarubian soldier jumped backwards and let go of the axe, unable to remove it from the back of his brother-in-arms quick enough. Darmour loosened his grip of the blade and let the dead soldier fall, diving on top of the other.

The two rolled around in the blood-congealed sand as each tried their hardest to gain the upper hand over the other. The soldier just about managed to overpower Darmour, but the pirate reached for a nearby rock in the sand and brought it down on the man's head, again and again, until he was satisfied that the soldier was no more.

He panted heavily and looked at Zerina, knowing he would fight for as long as he could, but understanding that his strength and energy levels were falling.

Zerina finished muttering her incantation and brought her arm up over her shoulder, waving her hands around at random. The speed with which she moved made it seem as though a circle of fire was forming around her. Then Darmour realised that it was.

Zerina sprinted towards the next line of Zarubians, a vortex of flame spinning around her. Her hair blew behind her as though she was in the midst of a tornado.

"ZERINA!" Darmour called after her. With no other option, he pulled his sword from the belly of the dead Zarubian soldier, raised his arm high, and chased after her, roaring his own battle cry.

Zerina stopped and slammed her foot into the ground, then brought her hands around to the front of her, clapping her palms together. The force of the magic was like nothing Darmour had ever seen as the flamed vortex surrounding her chased towards the Zarubian forces.

It hit them with a force they were not expecting. As flames engulfed their entire front line, wails and agonised screams hailed from the throats of the dying Zarubians.

Zerina danced in the sand, waving her hands fluently through the air, each gesture changing the direction of the deadly, flaming vortex. She clapped her hands together again, and Darmour looked on in amazement as the vortex split into two and moved in opposite directions across the entire line of soldiers. Her magic wiped out hundreds of soldiers in seconds with a wall forged from fire and the ash of their enemies.

The Zarubians faltered, their morale incinerated alongside their soldiers. Loud calls roared across the rear of their forces, commanding them to keep pushing forward.

Zerina looked strained under the force of her magic. Darmour could see thick, black veins protruding from her arms, yet she continued to channel her magic despite the toll it was taking on her. When the flames reached the ends of the front line, Zerina stopped and crumpled to the ground.

"Zerina," Darmour called as he raced towards her. He helped keep her steady. "You can't sustain magic like that, it will kill you."

Zerina had an angered expression on her face, one that she only wore when in combat. It was a striking change from the usual serene and caring woman that he knew.

"I will hold this line as long as I need to. It is the king that needs to fall on this day, not Levanthria's soldiers." She reached into her belt and removed the flask that contained the waters from the cursed fountain. Gripping it with cracked, trembling fingers, Zerina knocked her head back and tipped the last of the water into her mouth.

"Zerina," Darmour warned, "you need more supply of the water. Without this, you won't be able to cleanse yourself of the magic you use. Need I remind you the effect this has on you?"

"When the only other option is death, I know which I would rather choose," she said coldly. "You can escort me back to Treventine when all of this is done." The tracked marks on her arms faded as her skin returned to its usual freshness, the effects of her magic use reversed.

Through the flames, knights mounted on horses ran through. Darmour estimated that there were at least one hundred riders galloping towards them. They were not in formation, however, staggering their runs as they charged forward through the thick sand.

"Fuck!" Darmour cursed. "They are like fucking ants!" There were simply too many of them, and despite their best efforts, more and more continued to push through.

Zerina planted her feet into the sand as she started summoning her magic once more, a blast of magical energy engulfing her. Her jet-black hair danced around her as she screamed out in anguish, allowing her power to engulf her entire form.

"Darmour, step away from me!" she screamed as flames erupted around her.

The heat of the flames was enough on its own to force Darmour back, and he continued to move away until the heat didn't cause him too much discomfort. He still wanted to stay as close as he could to her, just in case. Not that he needed to or could offer her any protection; Zerina had proven herself time and time again to be anything other than a damsel in distress.

Darmour adopted a defensive stance, waiting for the cavalry to reach him. His chest heaved and his body ached, but as long as Zerina was of this world, he would continue to fight.

A sudden blast from behind them shook the very ground they stood on. A flash of light reached them first, forcing Darmour to close his eyes. Within seconds, an almighty noise boomed in his ears. What followed was a force of energy as if the wildest hurricane passed across the battlefield, flooring everyone who continued to fight. Ahead of them, the armoured knights fell from their horses, some crumpling underneath their steeds.

Zerina's flames were extinguished as she was sent rolling through the sand. The sky remaining bright as a large plume of magical energy shot into the sky from the crumbling keep, as if the gods themselves had chosen to strike it down.

Darmour rolled onto his back, the ground steadying. The sand clouds that sprayed out made it difficult to see ahead of him.

"They did it!" Darmour shouted at the top of his lungs, the windstorm around him still howling. "The Dwarf did it!" He clambered to his feet as the sand began to settle. Other soldiers did the same as they all stared back in shock and horror at the ruined keep. All that remained was a mass of rubble and stone from a blast of power of which the likes the world had never seen.

"Retreat!" a voice from the Zarubian forces called, and those that could began descending away from the battlefield as commanded, getting away from the chaos as fast as they could.

"The gods have struck," the same voice called. Zarubians ran past Darmour and Zerina, no longer interested in combat. Many chose to leave their weapons behind as they scrambled for safety from the powerful blast.

Darmour waded through the sand, which was uneven as new mounds formed at different places along the battlefield. Strange markings scarred the surface where the blast of air and energy had rippled outwards.

"Zerina!" Darmour shouted, unable to see her. "ZERI-NA!" There was no answer, and Darmour continued to desperately search through the sand for her. He continued his search until he saw a raised mound of sand and dust, an arm with tracked veins poking out from underneath. He raced towards her and slid to his knees, pulling on her arm as he rolled her out from under the sand.

She wasn't conscious. Darmour placed his hand on her chest and lowering his ear to her lips. He felt a faint heartbeat against his palm, followed by her warm breath against his cheek. He sat her up and pushed back the hair that matted her face as she blinked her eyes open, the effects of her magic already showing signs of wear against her usually unblemished skin. She was still beautiful though, and Darmour ran his hands through her hair again, stroking her cheek with his rough hand, his own chest thundering wildly.

"I thought – " he swallowed. "I thought I had lost you." He bowed his head and leant it against Zerina's, his hand still on her cheek.

She raised her hand delicately to the back of Darmour's. "The gods themselves couldn't tear me away from you." She smiled and sat up, pressing her lips against his.

27

Dust settled gently on Morvin's skin as he lay near motionless on a bed of rocks and mortar. His breathing was shallow, but he was still able to draw breath, even if every gulp of air felt as though he had swallowed glass. His body burned with an ache he had never experienced before, and his head throbbed like he had been trampled by a hundred wild zarulls.

Small rocks continued to fall around him as he lay at the base of the crumbling ruin, his dust-covered clothes sprinkled with patches of blood from his wounds. Morvin heaved himself onto his side, feeling every stone that pressed into him. With a grimace and a snarl, he tried to push himself up but let out an agonised scream as his right arm gave way underneath him. He had broken bones before, so he knew exactly what one felt like, but he had never broken his arm. Climbing to his knees, Morvin dragged his left arm up to brace his broken one as he planted his feet to stand amongst the ruins.

Coughing, he took in the destruction around him as dust continued to sprinkle down like a gentle rain. There was almost a calmness in the air which Morvin found disconcerting.

He looked around him, wondering how he would climb from the ruin and what the response would be outside. He had not thought what he would do beyond this point.

First, though, he needed to know if they had succeeded. He needed to know that the king was dead, and to achieve this, he needed to find his body.

Morvin's ears strained with a high-pitched ringing noise, everything around him sounded muffled and dampened. He stopped, sparing a moment as he thought about Skyrar. She had sacrificed herself in triggering the explosion. He knew there was no chance that they would ever recover her body.

"You did good, lass," he said as he stared down at the mountain of crumbled stone. A tear ran down his dirty face, leaving a clear trail in its path.

He needed to know the king was dead, however. He couldn't rest until he had the knowledge. Morvin dropped to his knees at what he thought was the epicentre of the blast and began pulling up stones with his good arm. He was in agony, but he needed to uncover the king's body. He needed to see for himself, and he would not rest until he did. He could hear the sound of people clambering from outside the keep as they desperately sought to get into the rubble, in sheer desperation, to aid the king.

Morvin continued to frantically dig, and with his shovel-like hand, he tore through the stone until his palm and fingers became bloody. Ignoring the pain, he moved as fast as he could, growling with each stone that he overturned and tossing them to the side.

"It is done?" a strained voice garnered Morvin's attention. "The king. Is he dead?"

General Precian emerged through the plume of dust, covered in dirt and blood. "No man can survive a blast like that," he said as he limped across the ruin.

"It is a good job that I am not a mere man!" a voice shouted.

Under a bridge of stone steps, King Athos Almerion stepped out from the ruins. He appeared ashen faced and in shock, and his face was bloodied.

Morvin spun around in a daze, his head whirling with the knowledge that they had failed.

"You will hang for this treachery!" King Athos hissed through gritted teeth, staring at the general.

Precian looked just as dumbfounded as Morvin felt as the king staggered out, reaching for his sword which was still clasped to his side.

"And when I am done, I will see to it that with the death of your family, your bloodline will run dry." The king only had eyes for the general as he rushed across the stone towards him. Precian tried to grab hold of his arm, but in his injured state, he was not quick enough. The king pressed his sword through the general's stomach and leant his head close to his ear. "There is a special place in the afterlife for treasonous cowards," he hissed before twisting the blade and pulling it out. The general dropped to his knees as his insides spilled out from his stomach. He looked on in shock, his eyes wide as he cupped his hands to catch what he could before collapsing to the ground.

"Now," the king snarled, "what do we have here. A Dwarf! Tell me, what role have you played in all of this?" He took a staggered step towards Morvin. "The general spoke to you as if he knew of you."

"You are a monster," Morvin growled defiantly. "Think of all the lives that have ended because of you, because of your god-forsaken war. You took everything from me!" A rasp in his voice stung the back of his throat as he challenged the advancing king. "You are no king, not to me. Because of you, I lost everything!" His rage built up inside him as he stared intently at King Athos, unmoving, unintimidated. If not for the king's actions, his dear wife and son would be alive, like so many others who need not have needlessly died in the name of his cursed war.

"God-forsaken?" the king quipped, his own face contorted with anger. "The gods themselves look down on me with favour. Morgana has foretold of me returning to Levanthria, with these lands and glory as my reward."

By now, Morvin had heard stories of the sorceress Morgana. It was hard not to know her name, given the power she wielded over Levanthria in the king's absence.

"Tell me, King Athos, did she foresee this?"

Their conversation was interrupted by Ulrik who stood on higher ground, looking down on them. He appeared as equally battered as Morvin. His clothes were shredded and blood covered his exposed skin, dust clinging to him like an unwanted mask.

Morvin's eyes widened as he looked up to see Ulrik holding Herelda in his arms. His legs were buckling under the weight, but he held her steady as he pointed it straight at the king.

King Athos looked on, confused by the contraption that Ulrik was holding.

"INSOLENCE!" he screamed as he charged forward with his sword outstretched towards Morvin.

With a click, Ulrik released a deafening blast from Herelda, the force of which propelled him backwards and out of sight. The blast of shrapnel met the king in his upper chest and slammed him down into the stone with a sickening force. Stone obliterated around him with another flash of light, another plume of dust rising into the air.

Morvin watched on in disbelief as the king writhed around in the stone, his blood flowing out of him like waves of an ocean.

He tried to speak, but only gargled rasps left his blood-filled mouth as he desperately tried to breathe. Morvin found himself conflicted, for they had done something unspeakable, and yet the revenge he had so desperately sought had been taken. The fact that he had not pulled the trigger himself was softened by the knowledge that it was Herelda that would steal the king's final breaths.

"You reap what you sow," Morvin said as he looked down at the choking king, who raised a hand towards Morvin, pleading.

"That is for Herelda, for Korvin. I hope the demons rip your skin from bone in the afterlife," he growled. "In fact, I hope all the souls lost by your command greet you there." And he stared down into the king's wide, blue eyes, until the light within them faded and nothing but a blank void stared back at him.

King Athos Almerion was dead.

Relief washed over Morvin. His chest beat hard, and his body ached as he continued to watch over the king's dead body.

"Come, we need to leave," Ulrik called, leaning down and offering a hand to Morvin.

Voices grew closer as soldiers advanced on the ruins, desperately looking for the king.

Morvin clambered up the stones, jumping as high as he could to grab hold of Ulrik's hand. Ulrik strained but was able to pull Morvin up over the ledge and help him to his feet.

"What now?" Morvin asked. All this planning, all the chaos they had brought . . . but now it was the aftermath, and it dawned on him that there was no plan for what came next.

"I think this belongs to you," Ulrik said. He picked up Herelda from the ground and passed it to Morvin.

"You did it," Morvin said. "You killed the king. It is over."

Ulrik stared down at the lifeless body of King Athos, and to Morvin's surprise, a tear fell from his face in a brief display of emotion. "Then why is it I still feel empty?" he said. "I thought it would feel different, bring me closure. Why is my anger, my hatred, still gripping me in a chokehold?"

Morvin didn't know what to say. Ulrik's reaction was not what he had expected of him. "We can't stay here," Morvin said. He could hear the footsteps of soldiers nearby.

"Over here," a voice shouted. "Send word. The king is dead!"

The voices came from below.

"You there!" the guard looked up at Ulrik and Morvin. "Stop them!"

"Go," Morvin demanded. "You have much to achieve in this life. I will buy you time."

"What about you?" Ulrik asked, almost hesitant to leave.

"You have helped me bring justice to my own loss, that of my wife and son. For that, I will forever be grateful," Morvin said, "There is a barrel of the powder I left behind on your ship, along with instructions on how to create it. See that it makes a difference in this world. Now, go!"

Ulrik looked downcast as he stepped away before turning and running out of sight, leaving Morvin on his own as soldiers climbed up from the ruins to draw level with him.

Morvin looked up into the fractured night sky and took in a deep inhale of breath. "Until I greet you both in the afterlife," he said.

With this, he let out a mighty roar as he charged at the advancing soldiers.

He was no longer just an inventor, but a warrior.

One that his wife and son would have been proud of.

EPILOGUE

T he king is dead. Send word to Morgana that he has perished in a plot to kill him from his own treacherous people. A force of magic and a device like never seen before was used to assassinate him. We will bring this very device back with us to try and reverse engineer it in the hope that we can harness its power.

True destruction has ended the war but at a great cost. For Levanthria now lies in a state of mourning. With no heirs, it is not entirely clear who will now rule our lands.

The Dwarf responsible for King Athos Almerion's assassination was apprehended and will be returned to Askela.

Report from Captain Fireya KR

JOIN MY NEWSLETTER

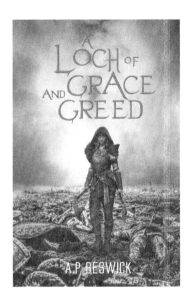

I hope you enjoyed this story. If you would like to keep up to date with my books as well as read one of my free short stories you can do so HERE

JOIN ME ON REAM

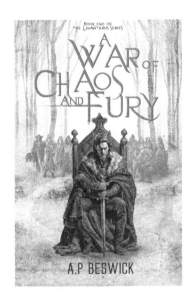

Join me on Ream to get early access to A War Of Chaos And Fury. You can join HERE

ALSO BY A.P BESWICK

OTHER BOOKS IN THE LEVANTHRIA SERIES

A Forest Of Vanity And Valour

A Sea Of Sorrow And Scorn

A Kingdom Of Courage And Cruelty

A Stone Of Destiny And Despair

A Frost Of Fear And Fortitude

A Loch Of Grace And Greed - Free Short Story Dust - Free Short
Story

A Forest Of Bastards And Betrayal - Short Story

You can get the best deals HERE

Coming Soon And Available For Pre-Order

A Frost Of Death And Deceit

A War Of Chaos And Fury